Stormsearch

Robert Westall

Stormsearch

Farrar, Straus and Giroux

New York

JF
WEST

Stormsearch

Chapter One

Mount House stands on a cliff. And on Mount House stands a weather-vane, shaped like a large spiky-finned fish. The fish is old. Old enough to watch Nelson sail past on his way to Trafalgar.

But to me, it was more than old, it was magic. For by a series of brass rods, gears and pulleys, it sent its message down through three cobwebbed, beetle-infested floors to a brass dial on the wall of the library. A dial marked not with hours, but the points of the compass; and one big black hand. When the hand moved, to tell us the wind had changed, it squeaked like a grasshopper. No matter how often Uncle Geoff oiled it.

It was squeaking now.

'Wind's backing south-west,' said Uncle Geoff. 'We're going to have a blow.' He tapped the great barometer, that only he was allowed to tap, because only he could mend it.

'Barometer's dropping. We're going to have a *storm*.'

He glanced at the tide-tables that hung beside the barometer. 'A storm on a high tide. Might find something interesting on the beach in the morning.'

I gave a wriggle of delight. Uncle Geoff could read the wreckage on the beach like a book; open it like a treasure-chest. This green, translucent egg was the bottom of a wine-bottle, ground smooth by a hundred years of sand. This rusty red spike was a nail from a French man o' war.

I listened to the wind rising. There is always wind round Mount House. The fish on the roof is never really still. But now the wind was tootling in the tall chimneys like a trumpet-player warming up. And throwing stuff against the thick small green windows that might be rain, or spray from the waves or sand or soil from the garden. The wind was starting to shriek as it nibbled at the corners of the house. The house was well-nibbled already. The coat-of-arms over the front door should have had mermaids, but they had been nibbled away to shapeless worms. Even the carved name below, MOUNT HOUSE, was the ghost of a name, only readable when the sun was in the west, throwing long shadows.

But we were safe, however much the wind nibbled. The walls of Mount House were three feet thick; you could curl up to read on the window-sills. A log fire burned in the grate, even if it was July. The fire spat viciously, as the rain came down the chimney leaving little black spots of soot on the worn stone of the hearth. In Mount House, on stormy nights, while your body was safe and warm, you could let your mind wander into sea-dreams. Even my sister Tracey felt it tonight. At home, she would boss her rag-bag collection of teddies and Barbie-dolls around, pretending to be a famous fashion-photographer. But tonight, she was voyaging into Narnia, turning the huge old leather settee into some stupid ship called 'The Dawn-treader' and ordering various crew-members to shin up to the yard-arm or walk the plank. I would not like to have been a member of Tracey's crew. The National Union of Seamen would not have liked it, either.

But was I any better, poring over one of Uncle Geoff's old books of maps, full of fat-cheeked cherubs puffing winds, and men with the heads of dogs running along the edge of the world and threatening to fall off, and the legend 'Hic Dracones' — 'Here be dragons'?

Uncle Geoff, on the other hand, was being wicked. He had brought the blackened works of one of his old clocks into the library, which was forbidden. He had spread a copy of *The Times* on the ancient glowing library table, to protect it from the sharp blackened oily metal. But every time he moved, the newspaper kept sliding off the table. Soon it would drop to the floor, and Uncle Geoff wouldn't notice, and by the time Aunty Megan came in, there would be oil on the library table, if not scratches, and then there would be hell to pay.

He was talking to the clock as he mended it, as if it was some naughty dog. 'Haha, *got* you,' he'd say to it, or '*That's* what you're up to, is it?' or 'Oh, no, you don't get away with *that*.' Lest you think he was totally mad, I must add that he was brilliant at mending old clocks. I have never known one beat him; people brought their clocks to him from miles around.

He disliked taking payment in money; he preferred to be paid in bits of old quaint machinery. Other old clocks, broken telescopes, bits of old duelling-pistols. Rubbish, Aunty Megan called it. But it was what he could do with the rubbish. He could make it live again. A broken flint-lock from a genuine old pistol, a length of iron Victorian gaspipe, and a lump of Edwardian mahogany bedpost, and he could make a duelling-pistol that could fool the experts. His jokes, he called them, for he stamped his name G VAUX clearly on the metal. But some of those jokes had once fallen into the hands of a dealer in Wolberton, who filed off Uncle Geoff's name, and sold them as genuine, and then there was *real* trouble . . .

Fortunately, Aunty Megan got in from stabling her animals before the newspaper actually fell off the library table, so there wasn't a row, just a loud and contemptuous sniff, then she sat by the fire and warmed her hands. She rides horses and teaches children to ride, and breeds donkeys, and although she has three huge sons grown up and left home, she still looks like a young girl, with her slim figure and pony-tail hair and rosy cheeks.

'Going to be a wild night,' she said, cheerfully. 'I think we'll have muffins by the fire.'

I gave a muffled cheer, and at the same time, felt through my knees and elbows (for I was lying full-length on the hearth-rug) the first really big waves hit the base of the cliff beneath us. It wasn't a worrying jolt; it was like when a train goes over points, or you ride your bike over a low kerb. It could happen all night, through your dreams, and Mount House wouldn't fall. You would feel it through the stair-treads as you came down to breakfast next morning, down the little dark winding back-stair, always known as Mary's stair, though nobody remembered who Mary had been.

An especially savage gust screamed at the house-corners, and something rattled on the windows that was more than sand or rain.

'Pebbles,' said Uncle Geoff. 'From the cove.'

'This is the big one of the year,' said Aunty Megan,

getting up to fetch the muffins to toast in front of the fire.

We were all enormously cheerful. How were we to know what was happening, at the base of the cliff?

Chapter Two

The wind was dropping by the time we came down to breakfast, and the tide was out, and the pounding at the foot of our cliff had stopped. The sky was pale but blue and weakly sunny, like an invalid recovering.

'Right; beach,' said Uncle Geoff, before I'd had more than one piece of toast.

'I want to come,' said Tracey. Uncle Geoff winced, and I groaned out loud. The trouble with Tracey is that she can't keep her mind on anything for more than half an hour at a time, and doing the wreckage on the beach would take Uncle Geoff and me all morning. She would get bored. And Tracey's getting bored was never Tracey's fault; it was the fault of anybody unlucky enough to be with her at the time. And she would make a slowly increasing fuss (starting with a gentle breeze and ending with a full hurricane) unless they did something about it.

'Come and help me with the donkeys,' said Aunty Megan quickly, trying her United Nations act. 'I'll let you feed and groom the new foal.' Which was a brill offer indeed.

'Oh, awright,' said Tracey ungraciously. 'But I'm coming down to the cove after.' Arthur Scargill has nothing on our Trace.

Uncle Geoff and I got out, with our big polythene

buckets, while the going was good, and whipped down the hundred steps to the cove.

The garden on each side of the steps wasn't showing signs of much damage, because it's mainly rocks, with pockets of soil in between where natural things like sea-holly grow, and other plants that can withstand the salt spray. But the white skull of Spartan the cat had been blown from its cranny beside the forty-fourth step, right across the stairs. Uncle Geoff picked it up gently, inspected it for damage, and put it back in its place.

'Why'd you keep it there?' I asked, for the hundredth time.

'Because that was his place for twenty years,' said Uncle Geoff for the hundredth time. 'He's entitled to his place.' And no more would he say, ever. No more than he would about Mary's stair.

But when we got to the beach, he gave a long whistle. The storm had made a difference there all right. More than half our sand had gone, leaving exposed banks of pebbles.

'The Lord giveth, and the Lord taketh away,' said Uncle Geoff.

'Will it come back?' I asked, awed.

'In time, I think. This last happened in 1968. It came back slowly, over the years. I reckon we'll not find much after all, this morning.'

But oddly enough, we did. Right on the high-tide line. (It was the outgoing tide that had stolen our sand.) We found things alive, and things dead. We found stranded jellyfish, dozens of them, including what looked like blown-up polythene bags with a few dark roots attached, that had once been the dreaded

Portuguese man-of-war, that can kill an unwary swimmer in deep water. Dozens of fragments of crab, both spider and ordinary. The gulls were scavenging the shore in a very savage mood, flying straight at us, before sheering off. We found a petrel, so exhausted that it lay quietly in Uncle Geoff's suddenly gentle hands. He put it out of the wind, in a cranny of the cliffs, and thought it was unharmed and would recover.

Then, out at sea, we thought we saw a loggerhead turtle swimming, that had been blown across straight from the West Indies — though we couldn't be sure, because we hadn't the binoculars with us, and the low morning sun was making the water shine, and it might only have been a young lost seal . . .

More to his liking, Uncle Geoff found a massive rusted ingot of iron, stamped with numbers, that he thought was eighteenth century, and might have been used as the anchor for a rowing-boat used perhaps by smugglers.

'Or just cargo from a sunken ship,' he added regretfully. He liked things to be thrilling, but he was much too honest to kid himself.

It was then that my dear sister Tracey arrived. And seeing the great shortage of sand, she of course immediately wanted to build a sand-castle . . . still, that at least meant that she had to go back to the house for her bucket and spade, and the other things for making a sand-castle. Which gave us another twenty minutes peace.

When she finally got back, she complained about the lack of sand, of course.

'Try under the headland,' shouted Uncle Geoff. 'There's still quite a bit left there.'

Grumpily, resentment in every step, she went. She

shovelled feebly for five minutes, and then came back to complain it was the wrong sort of sand.

'There's only one sort of sand round here,' said Uncle Geoff, a bit sharply. Tracey gets on his nerves, and he was trying to explain to me how lugworms feed and breathe.

'It's too *dry*,' said Tracey, stubbornly.

'Then wet it. There's no shortage of water.'

'The tide's out. It's too far to carry the water. Aunty Megan said I was to be *helped* to make a sand-castle.'

Uncle Geoff sighed deeply. Once the name of Aunty Megan was invoked . . . 'Would you mind?' he said to me, apologetically. 'I'll come and show you anything else interesting I find . . .'

Well, I had to, didn't I? She was my sister, my responsibility. Curse it.

Anyway, once we got settled down to it (and the sand was quite wet enough) I didn't mind too much. Uncle Geoff builds marvellous sand-castles, when he's not too busy. Towers with pointed roofs, using an old kitchen funnel, and even windows and buttresses, using lollipop sticks and bits of wood for supports. Even drawbridges over dry moats. And he's shown me how. And Tracey cheered up wonderfully, once she had me as her slave, and told me where to put the towers, and how not to spoil the drawbridge; and sang her favourite song, that she made up herself, and which only has one line, 'The flowers in the spring, tralala,' which she sings over and over again, till you could scream and go mad.

And actually, to be fair to Trace, she doesn't just get you to make sand-castles for the hell of it. Once they're half-built, she starts giving them names like

15

Castle Dread, and filling them up with imaginary people. Poor forlorn heroines, with names like Ermyntrude or Grizalada, who end up locked in dungeons full of skeletons. Men get a pretty rough time in her stories, being either villains with names like Barbarossa, or else hopeless wimpish heroes called Freddie, who only turn up to lay on a happy ending after Ermyntrude has saved herself by pushing Barbarossa off the battlements. She does all the voices herself, very realistically, as if she's forgotten you're there. I think she will be a famous novelist when she grows up, but more Jackie Collins than Mills and Boon. Uncle Geoff and Aunty Megan treasure her epics, and dine out on them at dinner-parties, which seems promising.

Anyway, I was doing Uncle Geoff a good turn, and he was never ungrateful, and he might find something totally fascinating left to himself in peace. He was at the far end of the beach by this time, stalking and pausing, head pointed down, like a great gaunt grey heron wearing a Barbour jacket.

It was then that the odd thing happened. I was digging fresh sand out of a pretty deep hole by this time, because although the sand-bank was deep, there wasn't a lot of it left. And at the bottom of the hole, my spade went 'thunk' on something wooden. From the sound, and the vibration through the handle, I could tell it was something *big*. Not just an odd bit of wood. My first thought was it might be a small barrel, buried in the sand.

'C'mon,' said Trace, 'we haven't got all day. Tide's coming in. I want two more towers *here*.'

'Trace,' I said, 'I think we might have discovered buried treasure.'

16

Forgive me. I didn't just want to shut her up. I wanted her to help dig it out. I must say the trick worked. She'd lost her faith in Santa at the unusually early age of three, but she still went a bundle on gold and diamonds, being female.

Anyway, she came to the other side of the hole, and we both scrabbled with our hands like mad. We soon got down to the first bit of whatever it was; about a square foot of it, curved both ways, like a barrel. But there was a sort of grey soggy canvas covering the wood, that was frayed to loose edges in places. And the grey canvas had black lines on it.

'It's not a treasure-chest,' she said in disgust. 'It's too long and thin. And what's this little bit sticking out?'

She fingered away the sand, and revealed a black spike of metal, about three inches long. It had a hole in its end, full of sand. And thin rings round it. And it was stuck hard in the curving wood. You couldn't even make it wiggle.

'It's a German *mine*,' she said accusingly. 'From the war!' She knew about sea-mines, because there's a harmless one on the seafront at Tynemouth where we live, painted red and used to collect pennies for the Lifeboat. And I must admit that for a second, I almost agreed with her. That big curving side, with the spike sticking out . . . but sea-mines had bigger horns than that. And they weren't made of soggy wood.

'Don't be stupid,' I said.

'I'm not stupid. What you're doing is *dangerous*. I'm going to tell Uncle Geoff on you.' And, in a moment, she was tearing off along the beach, waving and shouting her head off.

I sighed, and got on with removing more sand. She

could have her bit of fame. I wanted to know what I'd found, so I could tell Uncle Geoff when he arrived.

More curve; more soggy canvas; another black spike. Then my end of the object began to curve in sharply, and there was a rim of wood sticking out round the end of it. And a complex curved knob. I brushed away the sand frantically, and saw the curved knob was a little carved figure, with a twinkle of gold among the sand.

And suddenly I stood up, because I knew what it was.

It was a model galleon, buried in the sand. The spikes were its guns, and the little carved figure was its ship's figure-head.

And I began to wave my arms, too, at Uncle Geoff as he ran along the beach. My heart was in my mouth. I just knew that no matter if I lived to be a hundred, I would never find anything half so wonderful again.

Chapter Three

Uncle Geoff ran up with a 'what is the child going on about now' look on his face. Then when he saw what was in the hole, his grey eyes went very big, and then very long and thin.

'Crikey,' he said, and gave his little giggle. That's the funny thing about Uncle Geoff; he goes on half the time like a professor, and half the time like a schoolboy of forty years ago. Or so Aunty Megan says. Myself, I like the professor and I like the schoolboy. The professor teaches you things, but the boy's a lot more fun.

Then Uncle Geoff was down on his bony knees, scooping away more sand with his long thin hands.

'It's a galleon,' I said.

'Looks more like a collier-brig to me.'

Whatever a collier-brig was. But Uncle Geoff would know.

'Amazing,' he said. 'The stern windows are still in place. Real glass. And the rudder. Masts are gone, though. Snapped off when the waves rolled her over.'

Another five minutes of frantic scooping, and there she lay, exposed to the sun after hundreds of years, the sand starting to dry on her, and sand-fleas hopping around her deck. Over three feet long, and nearly as fat and round as a barrel. The canvas, that had once been stretched tight over her hull, now sagged full of pockets of sand, and gaped where it had torn.

'What was she covered with canvas for?' I asked.

'Keep her waterproof. Paint wasn't very good in those days.'

Then he glanced out to sea, and said, 'Hell, the tide!'

We all looked. The tide was returning up the beach, sending out long smooth sheets of water sweeping ahead of it.

I knew from building sand-castles and having them washed away that the waves would be here in quarter of an hour.

'We can get her up the steps if we're quick,' I shouted. 'I'll get Aunty Megan to help.'

He laid a hand on my arm. 'Quick nothing,' he said. 'She's full of sand. If we move her, she'll break.'

I went bananas, watching the long waves coming nearer and nearer. 'What can we do? What can we *do*?' To have found such a treasure and then to lose it was *unbearable*.

'Run up and get me a fence-post from the stables.'

I believed in him; to me he was a magic man, he could do anything. I ran.

When I got back, panting so hard I couldn't speak, there was no sign of the galleon at all. Uncle Geoff was smoothing back the last pieces of sand with his long fingers.

'Wha . . .?' I gasped. 'Wha . . .?'

He took the six-foot fence-post off me, and hammered it with the spade into the sand, at the edge of where the galleon had been. The heavy blows echoed around the cove like gunshots. He didn't stop till the fence-post was only sticking out about two feet. As he finished, the first thin wave swirled in round its base, and we had to scarper, to avoid getting our feet wet.

Soon, the waves were swirling six inches over the place; and then a foot, and then really big breaking waves, hammering down on the beach. I stood there, stunned, heartbroken. Already the galleon seemed like a dream.

Uncle Geoff put a heavy hand on my shoulder.

'Cheer up. We're coming back tomorrow. With *help*. A lot of help. I want every bit of that ship. Not just the hull.'

'Not just the hull?' I stared at where the fence-post had vanished under a curling breaker.

He opened his hand and showed me something small and black and rough and shapeless, about as big as a bean. 'That's a block-and-tackle from the rigging. You'd have missed that, wouldn't you? I want her masts and her sails and every piece of cordage. I want to know everything about her . . .' He looked as fierce as an eagle, as a judge sentencing someone to death.

'But *why?*'

'Don't you want to make her sail again? Don't you want to know where she was going, and where she'd come from? And whom she belonged to?'

'You can't,' I said.

'I can,' he said. 'Just try me.'

He didn't look like the kind calm professor now, or the giggling little boy. He looked . . . quite crazy in a calm sort of way.

He spent the rest of the day in his study, on the telephone, except for driving into Mountville, and coming back with a petrol-driven water-pump on the back seat of the Volvo, and the rest of the back filled with huge sheets of scrap polythene from the shop that sold spring-mattresses.

Aunty Megan explained to us that we weren't to bother him, because he was having one of his *things*. So I crept past him when I saw him standing in the hall at the foot of the staircase, clasping his high bony forehead with one hand as if he was trying to force some thought out of it. As I squeezed past, he said, 'Sieves, sieves, sieves.' Then he said, 'St John's Ambulance, of course.' And dashed out of the front door again.

We were sitting in front of the library fire, drinking our bedtime mugs of cocoa, when he finally came and sat down and agreed to have a cup of cocoa himself (which Aunty Megan said was a good sign). Then he gave me a keen sly look under his eyelashes, and held out his hand.

In the palm, something glistened, shiny golden. Something with two tiny turning wheels. About as big as a bean.

'Told you,' he said. 'Block-and-tackle from the rigging. Had it soaking in vinegar and salt. Came up good as new. Brass, you see. Lasts forever. Whoever built that ship knew what he was doing.'

That was when I began to believe the ship *would* sail again.

I didn't get much sleep that night, I can tell you. I heard Uncle Geoff's four great grandfather clocks chime twelve and one and two and four. I got up at seven, feeling like a buzzing bee, and had no breakfast except a mug of coffee. Then I was down the steps to the cove to join Uncle Geoff.

There is a platform about twenty feet above the sea, which is called the Spanish Battery. Uncle Geoff said it was either built against the Spaniards at the time of the Armada, or by some Spanish mercenaries to defend our bay against the Dutch, a hundred years later. It's nothing now but stones and a rather miserable lawn, because the grass won't grow properly so near the salt spray.

Anyway, this morning the miserable grass was covered by a multitude of objects. Not just the mass of polythene, and the petrol-driven pump and a jerrican of petrol, but a genuine stretcher, like they have in the sick-room at school, and a lot of sieves; gardening sieves and great big builders sieves that they use for sand on building sites. And a pile of trowels and old teaspoons and knives — half the contents of Aunty Megan's kitchen.

Uncle Geoff was watching the foot of the cliff through his binoculars. The sea was still up, and still pretty rough, breaking against the rocks and sending spray half-way up the cliff.

I knew what Uncle Geoff was watching for; the top of the fence-post. When it emerged from the waves, he gave a whoop like a cowboy.

'Right on time,' he said proudly. 'Right on time.' Then he looked at his watch. 'Time Tom and Jim and Barney were here, the idle sods. I told them to come early.'

I knew who Tom was. Aunty Megan's part-time gardener. And I knew who Jim was. The village builder, who came to renew the sash-cords. But as for Barney?

23

'He works at Exeter Boat Museum,' said Uncle
Geoff.

We waded out to the fence-post, while there was
still water sloshing round it.

'There's more sand,' said Uncle Geoff. 'Some of our
sand's come back.'

I groaned. More sand to dig away.

'No, it's a good thing,' said Uncle Geoff. 'More
sand rather than less. I was scared the sea would wash
everything away last night. Even the hull . . .'

I was glad he hadn't told me, or I wouldn't have
slept at all.

We began to dig while the odd thin wave was still
slopping into our hole.

'No time to lose,' said Uncle Geoff. 'We've only got
eight hours for the whole job.'

We found the top of the hull quite quickly, about
the time Tom and Jim and Barney arrived. Barney
had long hair and a beard and faded blue jeans, and
looked more of a country yokel than Jim or Tom.

After that, well . . . I didn't understand half that
was going on. The pump was set up in a big pool that
stays on our beach even when the tide's gone out,
because it's fed by a fresh-water spring. So we had a
hosepipe with running water; and every handful of
sand we dug was thrown into the sieves and washed
through with water. Anything solid left in the bottom
of the sieves was shoved into a polythene bowl of
water. I could see that some things were obviously
useless; things like pebbles and sea-shells. But Uncle
Geoff said everything had to go in; you never could
tell.

I was happy when the hull was exposed again; I felt
we'd at least got back where we'd started. But then I

was given the job of getting the sand out of the inside of the hull, which Uncle Geoff said was a position of great trust. It all had to go into the sieve, of course.

Half-way through the morning, about the time that Tracey escaped from Aunty Megan and began to hang around asking questions which nobody had time to answer, the hull was carefully lifted from the hole, gently wrapped in sheet after sheet of polythene, strapped to the stretcher and carried up to the Spanish Battery. The way they carried it, it might have been a person, a road-accident victim.

I understood even less after that. The hole in the sand was getting bigger and bigger, moving towards the cliff, and they were finding what looked like black broken bits of stick and rotting rag. Honestly, if you'd been beach-combing, you wouldn't have looked at them twice. But everything was left floating in polythene bowls, and Uncle Geoff kept having quick mutters with Barney about jib-booms and staysails and topsails and shrouds, and Aunty Megan came down with Mars Bars because nobody would stop for lunch, least of all Uncle Geoff, whose hair was full of sand, from where he kept running his fingers through it.

And then the tide was on the turn and coming back. We nearly left it too late, and had to run with all the stuff up the stairs to the Spanish Battery. Everyone was panting and swearing. And even then, they nearly left behind the poor little pump, still sending its stream of water down the sand. Jim rescued it (I think it actually belonged to him) and he was up to his waist in water at one point.

But they treated it all as a joke; they were in a very good mood with each other, as we carried all our stuff up the other seventy steps, and into the disused coach-house.

Uncle Geoff stopped on the top step for the last time, and watched the great waves overwhelm the poor fence-post.

'I only hope we've got everything,' he said. 'It's too late now if we haven't.'

Then we all went and had a drink, covering Aunty Megan's clean kitchen floor with sand, and even I was allowed a tiny wicked tot of whisky, and even Tracey a ginger wine. Then the rest went home, and I was sent for a bath, hardly able to walk.

Aunty Megan wasn't so lucky with Uncle Geoff. She said he came to bed at three in the morning, with his socks and hair still full of sand.

I was allowed into the coach-house the following morning; I think Uncle Geoff was a bit reluctant, but he did admit I'd found the thing.

The hull was on trestles, wrapped in swathes of polythene; the polythene was all cloudy with moisture, so it looked like a ghost in a shroud.

'Got to dry out slowly, or it'll warp and crack,' said Uncle Geoff. 'We may even have to damp it down again, if cracks start to show. But it's in marvellous condition — carved out of one huge block of oak. Must've taken months. No glued bits — the glue would have long gone, and all you'd have had was a collection of firewood.' He took off the polythene.

The hull was fat and tubby-looking. The ragged canvas still showed the patches of black and white, like Nelson's *Victory* at Portsmouth. And there were no less than 8 cannon, poking out through the bulwarks.

'Is it a man-of-war?'

'No, they were all painted like that. And they all had guns. To stop Frenchies and pirates cutting their throats. Nasty old place, the world was then. Even for the crew of a collier-brig. And in war, the Admiralty could take them over, as part of the fleet. Saved money. Quite handy really.'

He covered the hull again carefully, and took me across to a clear part of the floor. Here were laid out the rags and sticks of yesterday, with a mass of chalk-marks joining them up. The rags and sticks were starting to dry out.

'Doesn't that matter?'

'No — they're ruined. I'll have to make new ones — new masts and spars and sails and rigging. But I've worked out how tall the masts were, and how long the booms and spars and what size the sails. She was a top-masted schooner. You can see how she must've looked.'

And there, indeed, on the damp concrete floor, was the ghost of a sailing ship under full sail.

Sailing into our lives. After all those years. Bringing what? For some reason I shivered. But it was probably just the cold of the coach-house.

'Barney's taken some odd bits to Exeter. He reckons he can find out more . . . What the sails were made of. What kind of cord was used for the rigging. Look, we even found bits of that.' He gave me what looked like a thin brown worm. 'The sand's preserved everything wonderfully.'

But when I tugged at the brown worm, it parted under my fingers.

Suddenly, I did not like it in the coach-house. It was good to get out into the fresh air.

27

Chapter Four

The next ten days were sunny but boring. Because, as
Aunt Megan said, Uncle Geoff had gone broody as an
old hen. He was busy in his workshop, but the workshop
door was always locked, and when you knocked, he
shouted 'Bugger off' in an absent-minded way, and
went on sawing or drilling or turning. He missed a lot of
meals, furtively sneaking into the kitchen when he
thought no one was about, and shoving whatever he
could find in the fridge into a sandwich, then rapidly
sloping off again. Even at dinner he was late, and
absent-minded, drawing lines on the white linen table-
cloth with the end of his knife and muttering, 'That's
not it; that's nothing like it. Rubbish!'

But I know he was also on the phone a lot, and on
the third day, post started arriving from Exeter Boat
Museum and the Maritime Museum at Greenwich
and the Mary Rose Trust. Big fat bulging envelopes
and cardboard tubes marked 'Do Not Bend'.

Twice Barney came, and was let into the workshop
and stayed about three hours behind locked doors;
and on the Thursday Uncle Geoff was missing all day
and didn't get back till near midnight.

But on the eleventh day, as I was finishing breakfast, he came up and grabbed me urgently by the
shoulder.

'Need a sharp pair of eyes,' he said. 'A pair of sharp young eyes,' and whipped me off to the coach-house.

The great hull was unwrapped, out of its polythene sheets, which covered the floor and crackled as you walked on them. It was obviously a lot drier. It was no longer nearly black and shiny with moisture; more the colour of tobacco, with lighter patches; Uncle Geoff sprayed the lighter patches with a little brass garden-spray as I watched silently.

'It must dry *evenly*,' he muttered to himself. 'Evenly.'

Then he added, 'It's not cracked yet. The deck's warped, but that doesn't matter. You don't *sail* with a deck.'

Then he led me round to the stern.

'What do you see?' he asked. 'Look carefully!'

'The rudder,' I said, mystified, 'and two windows of green glass. One cracked. Captain's cabin, I suppose.'

'Right,' he said. 'Now you see that rough patch down below the windows — where it must have rubbed against the rocks?'

'Yeah.'

'Well, that's where its name should have been — if it ever had a name. But it's rubbed away, nearly. Now I want you to watch that bit very carefully. While I move this lamp.'

He pressed a switch, and a blinding white light hit the stern.

'See anything?'

'No, nothing.'

'Honest boy. Try now.' He moved the lamp to one side, more and more round to the side, like a setting sun. And on the stern, the shadows of the rough flaking wood changed and flickered. Then the lamp went too far, leaving the stern in darkness.

'Nothing,' I said, rubbing my eyes with the strain, and feeling a fool.

'Try again.' We tried again. And again. Nothing.

'Try a last time.'

He moved the lamp softly, to and fro. And suddenly there was a ghost of a name, in the thin shadows, and then it was gone again.

'B E N,' I said. 'On the left hand side of the stern. And I think there was an R at the other end.'

'Good lad.' His voice was a whiplash of joy. And I felt so proud to have pleased him.

'That's what I made it,' he said. 'But somebody else had to see it. I had to know I wasn't making a fool of myself.'

'So what do you make it?'

'Like a crossword clue,' he said. '-BEN---R' He sighed. 'And I spent all one day with the Oxford English Dictionary in Exeter Library, and the only word that fitted was EBENEZER.'

'Ebenezer?' I was disappointed. It seemed a rotten name for a sunken galleon. 'I thought it would be something like *Victory* or *Revenge*.'

'Those are battleships' names. "Ebenezer" is a good solid Victorian name for a good solid Victorian collier-brig.'

'Victorian?' Again, I was disappointed.

'Oh, yes,' he said. 'The sails were made of cotton. You don't get cotton in sailcloth till after 1851. It's flax before that. Big improvement — cotton holds the wind better and doesn't lose its shape. Barney found that out.'

'Oh.' None of it seemed very thrilling to me.

'But don't you *see*, Tim? We've got a name and we've got a date — we're on our way.'

30

'I suppose so.' It didn't seem a lot for ten days of Uncle Geoff being broody. I think he caught a hint of my feelings.

'That's not all we've got,' he said. 'Come and see in the workshop.' He covered up the hull loosely with the sheets of polythene, and led the way.

And in the workshop, I had cause to gasp.

He had sawn a length of wooden beam into the rough size and shape of the *Ebenezer*'s hull. And from this rough block sprouted two magnificent new masts, gleaming with varnish, and a new bowsprit, and a forest of new white rigging, with every little brass pulley in place.

'How . . .'

He gestured round the walls. Every wall was hung with plans of ships, blown-up photographs of ships, drawings of ships.

'What about sails?' I asked ungraciously.

'They're cut ready. They're in the washing-machine, being softened up. I'm keeping them in there for three days, to get the stiffness out of the sailcloth. Megan doesn't like it, but she'll have to lump it. First things first. You can wash clothes any old time.'

'So . . . we're all ready?'

'If the hull doesn't warp and split before next Tuesday . . .'

'Where will you sail her?'

'From where she came to grief.'

'But you don't know which way . . .'

'Oh, yes I do. Come and look.' He led me outdoors and to the edge of the towering cliff, and pointed down. 'See?'

I saw our poor little fence-post, still sticking gamely out of the sand, where we'd left it.

31

'Look,' he said. 'Look at the rocks which caught her.'

And I saw, as in a map, one great clutching arm of rock leading out into the sea, with our fence-post in the armpit of it.

'She was heading east when she foundered,' said Uncle Geoff. 'If she'd been heading west, she'd have ended up safe in our cove, on the high-tide mark, and someone would've rescued her the next day. That arm caught her, and the sea bundled her in, and rolled her over and smashed her masts to matchsticks, and buried her that same night in the sand. All on the same night. Otherwise, even there, the beachcombers would've found her, and taken her back to her owner for a reward.'

'Beachcombers?'

'Oh, yes. It must have been a terrible storm to have buried her that deep in the sand. The kind of storm that comes maybe once every two or three years, even on this coast. A storm from the south sou'west to the west sou'west, I reckon. Can't be sure. There'd have been more than her lost that night. Real ships, big ships, with people on board. The beachcombers, or wreckers as some call them, would have been out in force, after what they could find. You even got a reward for bringing a corpse ashore; from the coroner's court. Oh, nothing on the beach or the rocks would've been missed that morning.'

I shuddered. It was suddenly all too real, all too cruel.

'Makes our job a lot easier,' said Uncle Geoff cheerfully. 'I've got a list of the dates of the great storms, and when they blew and which direction they blew from. And we know exactly how her sails were

32

set, from the rigging we found. We found nearly every bit of rigging, you know.'

He went back up the path, whistling.

I thought historians were a very heartless lot.

On the Monday afternoon, Aunty Megan's washing-machine finally broke down, and she and Uncle Geoff had a fearful row, before he roared out of the drive in his Volvo and bought her a new one. Unfortunately, it wasn't the sort she'd had her eye on, and the plumbing-in would have to be changed and . . .

But all day Tuesday, Uncle Geoff was as sunny as the day was long. The hull had dried out and not split or warped, and he could start work on it. He went off after breakfast saying there was a lot of pitch painted on the inside of the hull, and a lot of lead in the bottom to ballast her, and it was all in a terrible cracked mess and would need sorting out . . .

He came back at lunch-time, still whistling and with the look on his face of a wicked pixie, and put a blackened tube on my place-mat as Aunt Megan was serving up the cauliflower cheese.

'Not *now*, Geoff,' she said, wrinkling up her nose. The washing-machine episode was still rankling.

'That's just in your line,' he said maliciously, shaking loose his napkin and tucking it into his shirt-collar to annoy her. 'A grand bit of romance. A grand bit of sentimental Victorian twaddle.'

He was not what you would call romantic, Uncle Geoff.

I picked up the tube, and turned it over in my hands, getting them quite dirty in the process, which did not improve Aunty Megan's temper. It was heavy, but hollow, brass I think, with a screw-cap at one end.

33

'Hand-made, that,' said Uncle Geoff. 'Nice bit of craftsmanship. Undo it.'

I unscrewed it with an effort, and I could see a little roll of something brown inside. I shook it out, and it flopped onto the white cloth, bringing a lot of little black grains with it. Aunty Megan's lips pursed further.

But I picked up the brown roll, and unrolled it. It was a sheet of paper, coiled tightly as a spring, so that it fought against my fingers. There was writing on it. But Uncle Geoff had to hold two of the corners before I could begin to read it. And of course dear Trace, and even Aunt Megan by this time, were peering over my shoulder.

'17th October

My dearest gentle Humbert

Today it must be! I have just read in the Exeter newspaper that our ship will sail one day early, having gained its full complement of cargo and passengers.

All is prepared. Faithful Alan took my box last night and buried it under the Admiral, in the place we agreed. It is not buried deep but the turf is replaced.

I shall ride in the park before tea, and come straight to meet you at the Admiral. We can have the box lifted as soon as it is dark, and await the coach. It is best done quickly, so we are not much noticed. The captain will marry us, I am sure, once we are at sea. I dream of our new life, under the Southern Cross.

All my heart for ever, my dearest.

From your ever-loving Henrietta.'

We all looked at Uncle Geoff. He gave one of his mad cackles.

'It's a fake,' said Aunty Megan. 'It's one of your rotten fakes.'

I must admit that my Uncle Geoff is a great faker. It comes from being clever with his hands, I think. And loving antiques. He thinks he can make anything. Once, he walked in with a lovely brass ceiling light-fitting, and said he'd just bought it at a sale, and what did Aunt Megan think it was?

Aunt Megan (who is no fool with antiques, and does a little dealing on the side at antique fairs) said she thought it was early Edwardian, about 1903. Whereupon Uncle Geoff doubled up and said he'd just made it that morning from two old stair-rods, a length of copper water-piping, and the knob off a brass bedstead. I remember she kicked him.

So when Aunty Megan said that the letter was a fake, we all looked daggers at Uncle Geoff.

But, maddeningly, he cackled again, and said, 'It's genuine. I found that brass tube embedded in the lead ballast at the bottom of the hull of our wreck. It's been under the sand for over a hundred years . . .'

And in the end, we had to believe him.

'But what does it mean, Geoff?' asked Aunty Megan, her cheeks glowing and her mouth open, showing the tips of her upper teeth. I suppose she is a bit sentimental, like most women . . .

'D'you remember that film called *The Go-between*? About a little boy who carried messages between two secret and forbidden lovers? Well, I reckon our good ship *Ebenezer* was used the same way — as a go-between. That's all it can mean, really. Her on one shore, and him on another, and her dad not liking the look of his face and forbidding him the house . . . and it looks like they were going to elope, but . . .'

'But what?' asked Aunt Megan.

'But that last letter never got there. It went down under the sand for a hundred years . . .'

'Oh, the poor things,' said Aunt Megan. 'I wonder what became of them . . .'

'I'll bet her dad didn't mind,' said Uncle Geoff, and gave his evil cackle again.

As I said before, I don't think he's romantic.

'I wonder what happened to the box under the Admiral,' said Trace. I could see she was sniffing after hidden treasure again.

'Oh, I expect they just dug it up again, when they'd got themselves sorted out,' said Uncle Geoff, as he turned his attention to his cauliflower cheese.

Chapter Five

That night, after we'd gone upstairs, Trace came to my room. She sat on the end of my bed, clutching her doll Violette in a rather dramatic way, like they were thinking of fleeing the country themselves. Trace is always rather dramatic and romantic at bedtime anyway. She wears these Laura Ashley nightdresses with romantic lace collars, and does up her hair in grown-up ways that would not be allowed in the daytime. And Violette, all of two feet high, is done up very Laura Ashley too. I wonder at Trace. She can't wait for her life to start getting romantic and tragic. She'll cause a lot of trouble for a lot of blokes, I suppose, because I have to admit she looks stunning, even if she is just a kid and my sister. I'm only glad I'm not one of the men she's looking forward to, that's all.

Normally, I regard these bedtime sessions as a pain in the neck; but that night I couldn't sleep either. My mind was in a whirl, too.

'Who *was* she?' beseeched Trace dramatically.

'Who?' I said irritatingly, pretending not to know.

'Henrietta. Don't start going on stupid, like Uncle Geoff.'

'How do I know?' I said, very off-hand, though I was mad to know as well.

'I thought you were supposed to be clever. Cleverer than me, anyway!'

That stung a bit, as she knew it would. So I put my mind to work. 'Oh, I'll find out,' I said airily.

'How?'

'Well, she was rich, we know that. And a rich Henrietta will be much easier to trace than a poor one.'

'How do you know she was rich?'

'She had that ship. And that would have cost hundreds of pounds to make. And she had a horse and a servant and a park . . .'

'She couldn't have a *park*. Parks belong to every-body. Anybody can go there . . .'

'Not in Victorian times, stupid. Public parks came later. This would be her father's own park, with a great high wall around it. That's how her father would keep her in, so she couldn't see Humbert.'

'A poor prisoner,' she said. 'A bird in a gilded cage.'

I don't know where she gets these dramatic phrases.

'How could her father stop her seeing Humbert? How could he stop her marrying him?'

'Oh, fathers were very powerful in those days. Especially if they were rich. Girls didn't go out to work — they were the property of their fathers, till they became the property of their husbands. Uncle Geoff told me. That's why girls eloped.'

'Oh, I know about eloping. Elizabeth Barrett Browning eloped — I saw that on the telly. She took her dog, because her father would've hanged it for spite — he was *horrible*. Then she was very happy, though she was ill. Then she died in Italy. It was so *beautiful* . . .'

Then her face lost its romantic yearning look, and

became as sharp as a needle again. 'Why wouldn't her father let her marry Humbert?'

I shrugged. 'Maybe Humbert had no money. Fathers liked their girls to marry money — make the family richer. Money always married money . . .'

'I would marry a man with no money,' she mused. 'After I get rich myself first. Then he'd have to do what *I* told him, though I would be very kind and thoughtful.'

'Poor sod,' I said.

'Just one thing strikes me,' she said, leaning her head on her hand thoughtfully, no doubt in the manner of Elizabeth Barrett Browning on the telly. 'What was a girl doing mucking around with a huge galleon like that? I mean, not many girls muck around with model yachts even now, do they? And it must have been much too big for her to manage. I mean, it's just not the kind of thing a Victorian girl would *have*.'

I must admit she bowled me over with that one. She was dead right. It *was* odd. But I just said, 'Maybe the faithful Alan helped her . . . he seemed pretty willing to do anything else for her . . . he was her servant.'

'How do you know he was her servant?'

'What else could he be — a rival boyfriend?'

'*Good-night*,' she said. 'I can't *stand* you when you try to be a smart-alec, like Uncle Geoff.'

I wished her good-night cheerfully. She was seldom so easy to get rid of. But afterwards I lay awake a long time thinking. I had to admit she'd hit the nail on the head, like she sometimes does.

What *was* a Victorian girl doing, mucking round with a huge model ship like that?

*

Now I must tell you about the Launch Dinner. It was held on the night before the *Ebenezer* made her first voyage. It was a pretty grand occasion. All the Vaux family silver was on display, and all the Georgian glass. And the old dining-room, with the family portraits, was lit by candle-light. Aunt Megan wore a long dress, and flew to and fro, worrying about the frozen whitebait. Even Uncle Geoff wore a decent suit for once, and what Trace got herself up as was nobody's business. I wore a suit, too, though I soon took the coat off, because the candles made the room so hot.

It was all the more amazing because Uncle Geoff and Aunt Megan weren't swankers with the things they had, like some I could name. I mean, they only mention the family silver when they're hard up and thinking of selling it. And they're very rude about the family portraits. There is one they call 'Bottlenose' and another they call 'Old Misery', who hangs in the downstairs loo. And most days Aunty Megan wears old jeans with horsehairs on them, and Uncle Geoff a sports coat that is thirty years old.

So it's a bit of a shock when they suddenly go grand. But then Barney had come, and his boss from the Exeter Boat Museum, and a man called Gulliver from Greenwich. And the *Ebenezer* was on the long Regency sideboard, with her masts nearly touching the ceiling, looking as big as a house.

The *Ebenezer* . . . how can I describe her that night? Brill? Fantastic? Magic? None of the words fit. I was supposed to be helping Aunt Megan, but I couldn't resist nipping every five minutes into the dining-room, to have another gloat over the *Ebenezer*. Her hull had a brand-new skin of canvas, brilliant in black and white patches above the waterline, and yellow-brown below to represent copper-plating. (The old canvas skin, torn and faded, now lay in a corner of the workshop like the skin of a long-dead animal.) The brass cannons shone like gold, the deck gleamed with varnish, and the masts and spars, and the snow-white of the sails glowed in the candle-light. And her name carved new into her stern, and on each bow, and picked out in gilt, like her figure-head and the carved scrollwork round her captain's cabin.

The men were impressed too, and clustered round her with their glasses of sherry, talking in deep reverent murmurs. I heard Gulliver say, 'She's unique. We'd have her off you tomorrow — we haven't got a good example of that type. But God knows what she'd fetch at auction. You've excelled yourself, Vaux. Almost seems a pity to put her in the water.'

I could tell Uncle Geoff was pleased. He looked for a moment like a solemn small boy. Then he bit it back and shrugged and said, 'She's a working sailing model, and she'll do what she was made for . . .' Then he added, 'The fore top-mast's the original, you know. And the topsail spar. I managed to save them. Good as new, after a hundred years under the sand . . .' As if the *Ebenezer* had nothing to do with him at all. He hates praise, like I hate school dinners.

The meal was very boring. The men talked nothing but shop. All shrouds and stays, companion-ladders and jury-rigs. Aunt Megan's eyes glazed politely, long before the cheese and biscuits. Trace said she had a headache and vanished. I sort of mentally came and went, feasting my eyes on that glowing ship and

41

dreaming . . . only one bit of their conversation do I remember. Gulliver saying, 'There's usually a logic in ships' names — every firm had its own speciality. The more educated shipowners went in for the names of Greek Gods — *Jupiter* and *Hercules*. The humbler sort named the ships after their wives and daughters — they often had as many children as they had ships . . .'

So, maybe we were looking for a family with a daughter named Henrietta and a son named Ebenezer . . .

I stared at the great model and fell into another day-dream.

The following morning, the weather seemed perfect. A blue sky, and a cool stiff southerly breeze. All the men had a bit of a hangover, but they seemed cheerful enough. We had plenty of hands to carry the stuff down to the beach; the hull strapped to that old stretcher, and Mr Gulliver carrying one mast and Barney's boss the other. All I had to carry was the boathook. Then we pushed Uncle Geoff's old rowing dinghy down the slipway out of the boathouse, and into the water. And Uncle Geoff got the *Ebenezer*'s masts and sails installed. Immediately, the *Ebenezer* seemed to come to life. Her sails billowed, and she moved on the sand with a creaking and grating noise.

'Let's get going,' said Uncle Geoff abruptly. It's not good for a model boat to have her sails set on dry land when there's a stiff breeze. You can strain something, because the boat can't move with the wind.

Barney's boss and Mr Gulliver hurried back up the cliff-steps. They would watch our progress through binoculars. With their pale summer suits, and panama hats, they weren't dressed for mucking about in boats.

Barney, on the other hand, was stripped down to a pair of bathing trunks. He was the deepest brown I've ever seen in an English person, and with his long hair and wild beard, he looked like a pirate about to board a ship with a knife between his teeth. Aunt Megan was wearing her old jeans, and Uncle Geoff his old baggy trousers. At least she had made him put on a clean shirt. I was in jeans, and Trace was in her bikini.

Uncle Geoff took the oars, and Aunt Megan and I sat in the stern, trying to nurse the *Ebenezer* on our knees. Trace supervised from the bow, and Barney swam alongside, all wet and grinning.

We got about fifty yards out into the cove, and shipped the oars. The sea was quite choppy under the breeze, rocking the dinghy. As soon as Trace got bored, she would allege she was getting sea-sick.

'What yer reckon?' shouted Uncle Geoff to Barney.

'Let's give her a go inside your cove,' shouted Barney. 'Let's see how she sails first. I don't fancy letting her loose in the estuary till we know how she handles.'

Uncle Geoff fiddled with the sails. The *Ebenezer* was struggling to get away from us like a living thing, as the breeze hit her. Uncle Geoff was swearing cheerfully under his breath.

And then gently, all four of us together lowered her into the water. It was good having Barney swimming, waiting ready to take her. She was *big*; four feet long with her bowsprit, and four feet six to the top of the mainmast.

Then we let her drift away out of our lee and . . .

43

The breeze hit her again. The sails filled like big white bellies. She heeled over sickeningly. I thought she was going to capsize.

Then she was off. A great arrow of water fanned out from her bow. Her lee bulwark dipped under the water, and a dark rill ran back over her hatch and little steering wheel. Then the lead ballast in her bottom forced her upright again, like one of those clown-figures that you push over and which spring up again, because they have lead in the base.

She went off at a terrific pace.

But she was erratic. She moved in spurts. The waves passing beneath her rocked her, spilling the wind out of her sails. And every gust that hit her drove her sideways towards the beach. God, she would be on the beach in no time, and there was quite a little surf breaking. Uncle Geoff began to row like mad. Barney began to swim like mad.

We all arrived back at the beach together; but not in time to stop the *Ebenezer* piling up on the sand with a sickening thump and capsizing over, looking like a real shipwreck.

They examined her as if she was a road-accident victim, but Uncle Geoff announced no harm was done, except a little gilt knocked off the figure-head.

We tried again. A hundred yards out to sea this time; and Uncle Geoff, after great arguments with Barney, set the sails differently.

It made no difference. She made straight for the beach again, like an express train. That time one of the shrouds gave way, as she hit.

'She's *rubbish*,' shouted Uncle Geoff. 'She'll never reach. She can't even run before the wind properly. She sails like a bloody fish-crate.'

Barney laid a soothing hand on his arm. 'Geoff —
what was the last model boat you sailed?'

'A modern three-footer, about four years ago.'

'Which had all the advantage of modern computer
design. And a big keel that held her steady. Geoff, this
ship is over a hundred years old. She may always have
sailed like a fish-crate. I swear you restored her
exactly, weight for weight, inch for inch. For God's
sake, be *patient*.'

'I'll *make* the bitch sail properly.'

'What — by fitting a great big modern keel?
Modern lightweight sails? Radio-control? Geoff,
where's your sense of *history*?'

'All right. You sail her.'

'Right.'

Somehow, Barney's hands were more loving. He
seemed to stroke the *Ebenezer* like a dog. The next
time, she sailed better. And the next time better again.
She got right to the end of the long beach of our cove,
to where, on the east, at the opposite end from Mount
House, Mount Head began its long journey out into
the Channel.

Barney looked up at us, shaking the water out of his
face. 'Not bad. Tell you one thing, though, Geoff. No
way is this boat ever going to get past the end of
Mount Head, in any kind of wind at all, north, south,
east or west. Anything south of west, and she'll pile
up on Mount Head; anything north of west, and she'll
go straight out into the Channel and never be seen
again.'

'So where was she heading, when she sank?'

'To your own front doorstep, boy. Or else somewhere further up your side of the estuary. And that's
all railway embankment . . .'

45

(The coast railway came out of a tunnel just behind Mount House, and followed the estuary round into Mountville.)

'That boat was coming to Mount Cove, Geoff. With its message. Anyone back in your family called Humbert?'

Chapter Six

Aunty Megan sat poised, with the teapot in her hand. 'Go and see if you can find your Uncle Geoff,' she said. 'See if he would like a cup of tea.' As she said it, she glanced at the big gap in the library bookshelves. The gap where the family papers and records had been stored, until that morning.

I thought her glance was a little nervous.

Uncle Geoff was off on another of his things. It was all Barney's fault, yesterday. *He* might have thought it was a joke, asking Uncle Geoff if there had been a member of his family called Humbert. But that was just the kind of thing to set Uncle Geoff off. He would not rest now until he had found out if there was somebody called Humbert. And when he was born and when he died, and whose son he was and whose father he'd been, and what he did with his life and what he died of. He wouldn't rest until he knew everything about Humbert it was possible to know.

Then he would probably write a book about him. Which might even become a best-seller. Like his book on the West Country wreckers, who lured ships to their doom in the eighteenth century by lighting false beacons on the cliffs. Or his book about Cornish tin-miners and their industrial struggles in Victorian times. Uncle Geoff chases a subject like a dog chases a rabbit, wrings every bit of life out of it, writes the truth and then, after the book is published, just shrugs and laughs and says 'Oh, *that* thing,' in a contemptuous sort of way.

'I saw Uncle Geoff drive off about three o'clock,' said Tracey. 'He went so fast he threw gravel all over the flower-beds, and nearly hit a lorry as he went out of the gate.'

Aunt Megan shuddered delicately.

'Go and look,' she said to me. 'He might've come back by this time.'

I don't know why she always sends me; but I went.

The trouble with being sent to look for Uncle Geoff is that Mount House is a big rambling place, full of holes and corners, and the out-buildings are more so. And Uncle Geoff sort of *spreads*; like dry rot. He had his workshop, and his study, and now the coach-house. And the hay-loft over the barn is full of the wrecks of grandfather clocks.

Typical of his spreading is the matter of the cavalry-sabres.

He is interested in cavalry-sabres; in every shape and improvement in sabres that was ever thought of. He brings them home as rusty wrecks, and does them up to perfection, then he wants to hang them on Aunty Megan's walls. Up the staircase, across the landing, clustered on the wall of the dining-room . . .

The trouble is, Aunty Megan is a pacifist. She doesn't mind the spread of grandfather clocks, except she doesn't like them chiming in her guest bedrooms. But the sabres drive her nuts, and then she puts her foot down. And Uncle Geoff meekly sends for a dealer from Stapledon, and the dealer goes off with an

48

armful, and the walls are clear again, and Uncle Geoff is left counting a huge wad of notes . . .

Until he goes out and buys another rusty heap of them. He has this need of them. He likes to say he has enough to equip a squadron of cavalry. Once, he went out to argue with a mob of yobs who gathered at his front gate, where there is a bus-stop to Mountville, and a bus-shelter.

Several of the yobs got nasty arguing with him, and finally pushed him over on his back. Uncle Geoff ran back up his drive, with the yobs killing themselves laughing . . .

Until Uncle Geoff re-emerged from his front door brandishing an unsheathed sabre, and yelling like a fiend.

They took to their heels, which was just as well for them. He chased them half-way to Mountville. I'm just glad they were younger and fitter than he was, and he didn't catch them.

Anyway, I went to his study first. I love his study, because besides the floor being littered with the insides of clocks, the walls are lined with shelves of model soldiers. Again, bought as wrecks and beautifully restored. A field-gun pulled by four galloping horses from World War I; a field ambulance with nurses spilling out of the back from World War II; Napoleon, double the usual size, on horseback, leading a century of Roman soldiers . . .

But Uncle Geoff wasn't there. The family records were, spread all over the big table, on top of the table's usual clutter, so that books and papers were suspended six inches above the table top. There was a huge brown crackly layout of the Vaux family-tree . . .

I soon found Humbert. Born 1845, died 1888. Son

of John Henry Vaux. Died unmarried, no children, in Winnipeg, Manitoba, Canada. And there was a photograph in an oval mount, faded sepia. A thin long face, with great big dark tragic eyes and long straggly and not very successful sidewhiskers.

Also on the table, open, was a big leather-bound account-book. The account-book of John Henry Vaux, written in firm beautiful clear Victorian writing. What was the connection?

I soon found it. Every month, the same item occurred, among the payments for the shoeing of horses and buying a new brass fender for the dining-room.

'To Humbert Vaux, ten pounds.'

The payments went on every month, from March 1868 till his death twenty years later.

I was still pondering when Uncle Geoff's car pulled up in the drive outside. I saw him get out, and he looked . . . sad.

Somehow, I stayed where I was. I just knew he'd come to his study first, before facing the family. And . . . I suppose I felt protective about him, he looked so miserable. I felt responsible. It was me that found the ship, and started all the fuss. And I was the only other family male present. And I am very fond of my Uncle Geoff.

He came in with his head down; looked up and saw me and said, 'Oh, it's *you*.' Grim, but not unfriendly. Then he threw himself down in the chair at his desk. I noticed he had a folded piece of paper in his hand.

He sat with his head down for a bit, then he said, nodding at the stuff on the desk, 'You've seen him, then?'

I nodded, not saying anything. He gestured at the old photograph.

'He was a bad Vaux. The rotten apple. One of the wild ones.'

'What did he do?' I knew about the good Vauxes, and the bad. My father had told me often enough; there was supposed to be a bad one every second or third generation.

'He was the town drunk,' said Uncle Geoff. 'The town drunk of Mountville. Brought home dead to the world in a cart three times a week. Fighting with the fishermen. Chasing the women. Then he got too big for his boots. Wrecking Mountville wasn't good enough for him. He went to wreck Exeter instead. Got in a fight with the town constables and threw one of them into the river. Even his rich father couldn't save him that time. It was Exeter, not Mountville. They put him in prison for a month. Drunk and disorderly and causing an affray. After he came out, the family sent him to Canada, and paid him ten pounds a month, on condition that he never showed his face in England again. What they called a "remittance man". The colonies, Australia, Canada, South Africa, were full of them. I suppose he drank himself to death in the end.'

He handed me the piece of paper, and I unfolded it. It was a photocopy of the front page of the *Mountville Guardian* for July 1868.

SQUIRE'S SON'S SAD FALL
THREW CONSTABLE IN RIVER AT EXETER
MAGISTRATE CONDEMNS THE EVILS OF DRINK

I read the rest of it. It was as he said.
He looked up at me with an attempt at a grin.

'Your dad thinks *I'm* a bad Vaux, you know. Your dad's a good Vaux, of course. I was a year older than him, but at school he was made a prefect first. Of course.'

My Uncle Geoff sounded very bitter.

'And there's your father running around saving the Third World from starvation, and here am I mucking about with model boats.'

I had tensed up at the first mention of my father. My father is a Professor of Agriculture, specialising in cereal growing. In vacation time, when he's not teaching, he goes belting around the Third World for the UN, trying to coax Third World governments into making two grains of wheat or rice grow, where only one has grown before. He's part of the Green Miracle, and my mother goes with him as his assistant. That's why Tracey and I come and stay every summer with Uncle Geoff and Aunt Megan.

My father has made me very tired of the Third World, over the years. Every Christmas, every birthday, every meal-time, the starving children of the Third World were dangled over us. How could I want a tape-recorder for Christmas costing forty pounds, like the other kids were getting, when that amount of money would keep a starving African child alive for four months? How dare I want an expensive birthday party, with a trip to the pictures? How dare I leave that food on my plate?

It came to a head when I was ten. I had left half my helping of my mother's cottage pie. My mother makes awful cottage pie; she's an awful cook altogether because she's too busy worrying or making notes or going to type something about the Third World. Food gets burnt; or she doesn't start supper until half-past eight at night, when you're starving and there's nothing worth pinching from the fridge.

I left that cottage pie.

My father said, 'Some child in the Third World would be very grateful for that.'

I rushed out of the room with the plate in my hand. I ran to my father's study, and got one of his big used padded envelopes, and I stuffed the cottage pie into it with my fingers. Then I scrawled the address of UNICEF on the enevelope with a great big felt-tip, and went back into the dining-room and handed him the whole mess.

He didn't say anything. Neither did my mother. But they both went very white. Mind you, they didn't hit me or anything. They're not into corporal punishment. They just glare at you; go all icy and speak to you like you were an infant Hitler; shut you out.

Things hadn't been the same between me and my parents since then. I'm outside, now, and I'm never going to get back. I suppose if I starved myself until my legs were like sticks and my belly stuck out, they might take an interest. I couldn't care less.

Mind you, they still do their best for me. What *they* think is best for me. But it's a great relief to get to Uncle Geoff's and Aunt Megan's for the whole summer.

Now, I looked at Uncle Geoff. His face was different; I think he must have been watching the expressions change on *my* face.

I said, 'I don't think you're a bad Vaux. The *Ebenezer* is marvellous. Gulliver doesn't think you're a bad Vaux. Your publisher doesn't think you're a bad Vaux . . .'

He nodded at the old photograph on the desk. 'What about him then?'

'I like his face. He looks . . . kind. He looks as if he wouldn't hurt a fly. What did he do, before he became the town drunk?'

'He was an undergraduate at Oxford. He got a very good degree in Mods and Greats. He came home from Oxford intending to become a vicar. He wrote some quite decent poetry; like a young Matthew Arnold.'

'Something changed him.'

'So you think,' asked Uncle Geoff, 'that he was a good Vaux until something made him into a bad Vaux?' He was teasing me now, and yet there was a seriousness behind the teasing.

'Yes,' I said.

'Well, you and I shall have to find out what changed him then, shan't we?'

You and I. That's the great thing about Uncle Geoff. He's either far away from you, or very close to you, depending on his mood. But when you've got parents who're never close to you at all . . .

'Let's go and tell Aunty Megan,' I said. And added as an afterthought, 'and Trace, of course.'

We went through to tea together, like two conspirators, his hand on my shoulder. And Aunty Megan and Trace greeted us like fellow conspirators, with relieved grins and fresh tea in the teapot.

Trace fell in love with the photograph of Humbert on the spot, asked Uncle Geoff if she could keep it in her bedroom. He said she could, suppressing a smile, and cocking one eyebrow at Aunty Megan while Trace was poring over the bit of sepia and positively drooling.

And then she amazed us. She suddenly said, 'I know where there's another picture of him. He's hung on Mary's stair. Half-way up.'

Then we all had to rush up Mary's stair, and there he was: a biggish oil-painting, showing him down to the waist. On a cliff-top in a big open coat, and the coat and his hair and sidewhiskers blowing in some great gale. And beyond the cliff, out to sea, a wreck of a sailing ship, aground on some rocks, with the waves breaking over her . . .

'There's a story behind that,' said Uncle Geoff. 'That shipwreck's not there by accident . . .'

'I think he must have done something very brave,' said Trace. 'And town drunks can't do something very brave. They couldn't stand up straight long enough.'

Which sent us all back to the library in a good mood.

'Anyway,' said Uncle Geoff. 'We've narrowed the years down a bit. Whatever happened, it happened between 1851, when that cotton sailcloth was first made, and 1868, when he left for Canada.'

'I've thought of something else,' said Trace importantly.

Having grabbed us all by the lugholes, she took her time.

'I still want to know why Henrietta's father wouldn't let her marry Humbert.' She turned on me. 'You said maybe it was because he had no money. But if he was Humbert *Vaux*, he must have had pots of money.'

Uncle Geoff and Aunty Megan fell about laughing, at the idea that all Vauxes must have pots of money. But Uncle Geoff said, 'He was the eldest son; and the heir, till he fell into disgrace. He would have had pots

of money when his father died. Most men would have grabbed him as a son-in-law . . .'

'Well, we know all about Humbert now,' said Aunty Megan. 'Now we must find out all about Henrietta. I'm sure you can do it between you.'

Chapter Seven

Uncle Geoff called to me from the open door of the church vestry.

I'd been wandering in a daydream. Mountville church was a really smashing place, especially towards sunset. There's stained glass in all the windows, and the sun splashes through in great pools of light — red, blue, green, purple — that lie on the dusty stone slabs of the floor, and climb up the pillars, and lick across the great white marble tombs, of sea-captains, West Indian merchants, ship's chandlers and their wives and daughters. The tombs are covered with beauti-fully-carved figures: sailors resting their elbows on anchors; admirals leaning against heaps of marble cannons, cutlasses and boarding-pikes; weeping full-bosomed nymphs holding up oval plaques of their dead heroes. Very dusty, but very intriguing. Makes you wonder what kind of heaven the sailors and merchants and ship's chandlers thought they were going to.

I was supposed to be looking for Henrietta; I *had* been looking for Henrietta at the start; hoping every full-bosomed nymph might turn out to be her. But I'd looked everywhere, on every memorial, and I only had two Henriettas, and they were quite useless.

'What've you got?' asked Uncle Geoff, wearily.

'Henrietta Young, a widow of Impregnable Chastity and Great Piety died 1790,' I said. 'What does Impregnable Chastity mean? Makes her sound like a castle or a battleship.'

'Means she didn't have any more boyfriends, once her husband died. Or at least nobody caught her out with one,' said Uncle Geoff. 'What else?'

'Henrietta Champney, dearly beloved only daughter, died at seven and a half in 1767.'

'Too small to sail boats or have boyfriends,' said Uncle Geoff. He did sound so weary, so I said sympathetically, 'No Henriettas?'

He held up the last of the parish registers. Its cover was a dingy grey, a bit like unwashed human skin.

'Too many bloody Henriettas, born, wed and died. But they were born to fishmongers, or safely married to tin-miners, or the widows of paviours. Or they were babes in arms, or had one foot in the grave, at the time when brave Humbert was a-roving by the light of the moon. Here *and* in the County Record Office. And that's the lot. She might as well never have existed.'

'Well, at least we tried,' I said.

'The trouble is we just don't know enough. All we know is that she was called Henrietta, and was of eloping age, and had a rich dad with a park, somewhere the other side of the estuary. If only we had a surname!'

'Are you going to give up?' It would not be at all likely for him to give up.

He gave me a quick glance from under his eyebrows, and his sudden shark-like grin of jolly malice.

'No, we'll play the wild card. We'll make proper

fools of ourselves. I'll ask Barney over, when the winds are right, and the *Ebenezer* will sail again. Maybe she'll lead us home. It'll be a nice day out, anyway!'

So there we sat, in Uncle Geoff's big old rowing-boat, bobbing on the gentle waves of the cove again, with the *Ebenezer* on our knees. Trace was in the bow, in her bikini, because the sun was shining, and even the southerly breeze was hot. Aunty Megan was in her bikini too. Uncle Geoff and Barney were sitting on the middle thwart, where you do the rowing from. Barney was in his bathing trunks, and browner than ever; and Uncle Geoff was wearing his baggy old grey trousers and a shirt with varnish-stains down the front.

Uncle Geoff and Barney were arguing, as usual, half-matey, half-sharp, like two fox-cubs having a scrap.

'It's the only storm between 1851 and 1868 that fell on the 17th of October. 1866. An early equinoctial gale. Look, it's here in the Coast Guard weather records.' He produced a crumpled wad of photocopies from his back pocket.

'Weather fine and clear visibility till eleven am. Wind due south, a steady breeze. At eleven, a sudden squall, still from the south. At seven pm, the wind backed south-west and increased to severe gale force rapidly. That sudden squall must have been the one that did for the *Ebenezer*. You know how strong wind blows her sideways. It put her into those rocks. The severe gale would have buried her under the sand later as she lay helpless . . .'

'All right, if you say so, squire! What you want to do?'

'Let's take her out into the estuary, and sail her round our headland, past the rocks, into our cove!'

'Your every word is my command!' Uncle Geoff and Barney began to row, side by side, one oar each. They couldn't even *row* without squabbling over who was pulling on their oar too hard.

We got out into the middle of the estuary.

'This'll do,' said Uncle Geoff. He glanced up and down the estuary. 'All clear. Nothing coming.'

There wasn't another vessel in sight, except for the gaggle of weekenders' yachts moored far up, near the quay at Mountville. The estuary had been a busy harbour once. I've seen old photographs, with sailing-ships moored three abreast. China-clay boats in for repair, collier-brigs from South Wales, coasters full of potatoes for London, packet-boats waiting for passengers . . . Now there were just five sturdy tub-like fishing-boats, with tripod masts and smoky diesel-engines, that were usually gone as soon after dawn as possible. And the weekend sailors only bothered us at weekends . . .

'Right.' Barney's long brown fingers moved over the rigging of the *Ebenezer*. He looked like a guitar player tuning his guitar; except guitar players are not alive to the strength of the breeze playing on their cheeks and through their hair and beard. Their eyes do not narrow and see every catspaw on the gleaming water, every breeze coming and going and dying on the ripples; every wind-shadow where the wind does not come, and the water lies smooth and darkly reflecting under the cliffs. My uncle was a great model-maker, and he knew how the mainsail of the *Ebenezer* must be set, and how the foresail had to be set to

60

balance it. But Barney was a real old salt at thirty, a deep-water sailor who'd crewed on the *Sir Winston Churchill* in gales, and sailed American schooners in the West Indies. He'd risked his life with wind and wave and tide. He *was* the sea and the ship. And he knew deep down how to set the *Ebenezer*'s smaller sails, the square-rigged fore-topsail, and the stay-sail and the jib, so they would all pull together. There, my Uncle Geoff didn't have a clue.

'Right,' said Barney again, and we carefully lowered the *Ebenezer* into the water, and backed away.

The wind took her; her masts dipped, her arrow-like wake grew, and she was away. She was sailing beautifully, every sail calm and solid with wind, 'asleep' as the sailors say. No fluttering, no flapping. The incoming waves still made her sway as they passed under her; but less than they used to. Hardly any wind was spilt out of the sails. Every bigger gust blew her towards our cliff, and the rocks below; but in between she recovered, and gently sliced back out to sea again.

She passed the outreaching rocks that had caught her so long ago, with ten yards to spare, and we all cheered her like mad. Then we had to row like hell to keep up with her, as she gently headed for the far end of our beach, under the bulk of Mount Head.

We caught her just before she beached, and no harm done.

'She's very fast,' said Barney, looking up with a white-toothed grin, his brown face all spray. 'What now?'

'Let's put her into reverse,' said Uncle Geoff. 'On the reciprocal course. Let's see if she'll take us home.'

Barney fiddled some more, altering the sails. And then the *Ebenezer* was away again, back towards the estuary. Our hearts were in our mouths again, as she rounded our headland and the rocks that had been her grave. She missed the rock by less than three metres that time.

'Breeze is getting up,' said Barney. 'Row like hell.'

Because, once clear of the rocks, as the high-banked estuary began to funnel the wind stronger, the *Ebenezer* really flew. As if she was glad to be going home. Like a dog streaking back to its master . . . mistress. For all that voyage of two hundred yards, across the estuary, we were in the grip of some weird excitement. Trace was screaming her head off in the bow; Uncle Geoff and Barney gasping over the oars; Aunty Megan uttering incoherent cries of sympathy, wild as a sea-gull, urging the *Ebenezer* on. And I, I was lost in a dream, in which time meant nothing. The *Ebenezer* was going home, through space and time . . .

We just caught her before she reached for the further shore; we caught her because, for the last twenty yards, she went into the wind-shadow of the far bank, where the water lay smooth as a mirror, and the breeze did not come, and the *Ebenezer*'s masts slowly came upright, and the arrow of her wake dwindled to one tiny ripple, then died. She bobbed upright, and was still, almost like a puzzled dog, baffled of her prey.

We looked up, and really *saw* the further shore, for the first time.

I have never felt such disappointment. I was looking for what? A walled park? A great house? A girl sitting on her horse on the shore, with her personal groom waiting respectfully on his horse behind? Ghosts?

What we saw were bungalows. Rank upon rank of bungalows, climbing up the steep hill. Nasty little bungalows, the worst sort of bungalows, with odd-shaped chimneys in funny bumpy stone, and roofs of garish blue and green tiles. And cars outside garages, and caravans parked on hard-standings and potty little aluminium-framed greenhouses, and someone with a tranny by their sun-lounger, playing Radio One.

I suppose you could say we should've known. But the far shore had always looked quite attractive from our shore, because trees had been left among the bungalows, and the bungalows, with their white walls had just looked like an extension of the old white-walled town. And there'd usually been the blue haze of distance, or the sun had been setting and the bungalows had been in shadow. It wasn't a part of the town Uncle Geoff had ever taken us to. It wasn't a part he ever went to. He only liked historical things . . .

'God,' said Aunty Megan. 'It looks like the worst bits of Majorca. Why do they let people build such things?'

'I suppose people have got to live somewhere,' said Uncle Geoff miserably. 'Perhaps they actually *like* living here.'

'Maybe I set the sails wrong,' said Barney apologetically. 'Or the tide was setting differently. The tide can make a hell of a difference . . .'

'Now we're here, we might as well explore,' said Uncle Geoff. 'Let's get the *Ebenezer* on board.'

We lifted her, and she sat across my knees and Aunty Megan's in the stern, dripping. The others rowed up towards the quayside at Mountville, and we passed a succession of blue-rinsed ladies hanging out washing or sunbathing, and elderly gentlemen, with bare bony chests showing sun-reddened between their panama hats and striped Bermuda shorts, busy dead-heading roses or cutting privet. They stared at us even more grumpily than we stared at them. We must have been a rather odd sight.

We rowed all the way to where the quayside and docks began, just to make sure there was nothing. There was nothing older than 1950 at the earliest. Then we rowed all the way back, and it was hard work because the tide was really setting-in now. We rowed all the way to where the sheer stone cliffs sprang from the sea, under the towering walls of Mount Castle. Nothing.

'Let's go home,' said Aunty Megan.

'Yes,' said Trace. 'I feel sea-sick.'

But just as we were turning, Uncle Geoff said sharply, 'What's *that*?'

We rowed towards whatever it was.

A row of stumps were pushing themselves a couple of feet above the waters of the estuary. They were rather pretty, for the old thick wood had rotted, and odd plants had sprouted from the cracks. Tufts of grass; a plant with yellow flowers, a plant with blue flowers. They looked like miniature tropical islands in the estuary. I imagined a model yacht (much smaller than the *Ebenezer*) sailing from one to the other; with model soldiers aboard. Sailing to these Islands of the Blessed . . .

'There's been a landing-stage there, at one time,' said Uncle Geoff. 'With steps down.' He pointed to a diagonal piece of wood, still bolted to the end upright. 'And here's a mooring ring . . .' He dug out, from under a mass of flowering moss, an old iron ring red with rust.

'Just a bit of the old quay,' said Aunty Megan.

But Barney shook his head, and Uncle Geoff said, 'Too small for sailing-ships. Too far from the main quayside. This is a place for ... pleasure-craft — a little steam-launch at most. A private jetty. Let's row into the shore ... look, there's the remains of steps cut in the bankside ...'

Suddenly, he stood up; and launched himself without warning at the shore. Slipped, nearly fell in the water, grabbed a tuft of grass and saved himself. The boat rocked horribly at his going, nearly tipping the *Ebenezer* off our knees and back into the water. Everybody shouted at him angrily. But he couldn't have cared less.

'There's a big old slab of concrete. There's been a shed here at one time. I think we're onto something. *C'mon!*'

Such was the excitement in his voice, that I launched myself after him. There were more angry shouts from the boat. And I *would* have fallen in, if Uncle Geoff hadn't reached down a big hand and grabbed me.

I looked back. The rowing boat was drifting away, under the force of my jump.

'Row back home,' shouted Uncle Geoff at the three semi-naked figures sitting in it. We'll join you later.'

'Thanks very much!' shouted Aunty Megan.

We had to trespass up somebody's garden to get to the road; and since the somebody was there, mowing his back lawn, it wasn't a happy beginning. I think he took us for a pair of lunatics, and was thinking of calling the police. Especially as all Uncle Geoff seemed to think of to say was 'What's the name of this road?

The name of the road you live in, man? *That* can't be difficult!'

We got away without the man dialling 999 in the end.

The name of the road was 'Riverside View'.

'That's no use,' said Uncle Geoff.

The next road, going up the steep hillside, was called 'Hillside View'.

'That's useless, as well,' said Uncle Geoff. And 'Riverside Crescent' and 'Riverside Close' were equally unsatisfying to him. As were 'The Moorings' and 'Moorings View'. In fact, there seemed nothing in all that dreary endless vista of tiny bungalows that made him happy at all. Until we came to 'Owen Avenue' much further up the hill, where the land was flattening off.

'Ha!' said Uncle Geoff. '*That's* interesting.'

'Why?' But he didn't answer. Just quickened his stride like a great heron stalking along, so it was very hard to keep up with him.

And 'Gower Avenue' excited him even more. He was practically running by that time.

And then we came to 'Gower Park Road' just as the road turned down off the hill of bungalows towards the town centre of Mountville.

'"Gower Park Road,"' said Uncle Geoff, with simple happiness, as if he had just arrived in heaven. '"Gower Park Road."'

'What's so marvellous about "Gower Park Road"?' I asked grumpily. I was very hot and very thirsty, and was just realising what a long walk it was going to be back to Mount House, right through the town centre. And if I knew Uncle Geoff, he wouldn't even have any money in his pocket to pay for a bus-fare.

66

'Gower Park Road,' said Uncle Geoff, 'means the road to Gower Park. And the Gower is a place in South Wales, and then we have "Owen Avenue" and "Owen" is also a Welsh name.'

'So . . . ?'

'We were looking for a rich man's park, with a wall around it, and we've found it.'

'Where's the wall?' I shouted rather rudely.

'Can't you use your eyes, boy? The wall is right in front of you.' He pointed with his foot.

The garden wall of the nearest bungalow, only about three feet high, was built of huge, beautifully carved stone blocks.

'You don't think the jerry-builder who built these rotten bungalows could afford those kind of stones, do you? They must have been here before he started building. He just used them because they cost him nothing, because they were here already. Just like these great trees, dotted around the gardens. They were here long before the bungalows, too. Two hundred years old. Chestnut, oak, beech. Rich man's trees. Trees in a rich man's park. Gower Park. Owned by the Owen family, or my name's Adolf Hitler. The Owens of Gower Park, boy. It's all still here. Only, some time in the 1950s, some builder bought the Park and built his rotten bungalows all over it. We've found her, boy, we've found her. I'll bet you a pound to a penny, our heroine's name was Henrietta *Owen*.'

I think he would have danced with me there, in the street, if there hadn't been people watching from behind their privet hedges and lace curtains.

Chapter Eight

Next day was another day without Uncle Geoff; he was gone before we got up; Aunty Megan said he'd gone off as happy as a cat with two tails.

He arrived back when we were having tea on the terrace, and announced 'Come and see' with the grin of a boy who has just built the best sand-castle in the world. Aunty Megan knew there was no arguing with him in *that* mood. She came straight away (though she did bring her cup of tea with her).

He led us to the old coach-house again. The *Ebenezer* was still there in the middle, on her stand. She looked a little battered, a little salt-stained in the sails. Her shiny brass guns had gone dull. But she looked a lot more *real* somehow. A working ship.

But all the other pictures and plans of working collier-brigs had gone from the walls. Instead, a new set of hugely enlarged photocopies were pinned up. Uncle Geoff knew a shop in Exeter, where they did huge enlargements. He spent pounds there.

He gestured at a map of the whole area round Mountville.

'Gower Park,' he roared. 'Gower Park, just where I said it would be. That's the Ordnance Survey Map of 1872. And here's an enlargement, shows everything — park wall, the great house, orchards, formal gardens, orangerie, tenants' cottages, everything. Even that little pier with the steps and the shed we found yesterday.'

But none of us said congratulations. We were all looking at a face pinned next to it on the wall. Another huge enlargement — so huge that, close to, it just broke down into a series of dots and splodges of black. The face of an old man, almost the face of a skull. White tufts of hair clung to the shiny bald head. The eyebrows were thin too, and the little eyes nestled deep in the sockets, like black snakes looking out of pits. The lips were clenched so tight you could tell he had hardly any teeth left, yet you felt that what teeth he still had would give you a nasty bite. So old, so merciless, so sure he was right. I would have been frightened of him, even after he was dead. Especially after he was dead.

'I don't like that face,' said Trace. 'He's watching me.'

And even Aunty Megan shuddered. 'Who was he?'

'Alderman Idris Owen, of Gower Park. From the Mountville year-book of 1899,' said Uncle Geoff. 'Our great public benefactor. Built the Mountville Public Baths and the Mountville Library. Started life as a ship's boy, on the collier-brigs bringing coal from Swansea round the coasts of Cornwall and Devon. Rose to be captain. Saved enough to buy his own ship, when times were bad, and the coal-trade slack, and collier-brigs cheap. After that, he bought ships when they were cheap, and sold ships when they were dear. Made a fortune. Owned his own coal-mines, and in middle-age settled in his favourite port of call, Mountville, and built himself his great house at Gower Park.'

He pointed to a third huge enlargement; an engraving this time; the tiny engraver's marks had been enlarged till they were as big as blades of black grass. 'Gower Park in its heyday.'

It stood on the crest of its hill, above the estuary. It looked like a Gothic cathedral that had gone wrong, and grown like a black cancer down the slope. Buttresses, pinnacles, great ornamental windows. And above all, the tower, far too high for the rest of the building, nearly as thin and high as a factory chimney.

'That was *his* tower,' said Uncle Geoff. 'From there he could watch everything through his big brass telescope. Just like he was still the captain of the ship. His collier-brigs coming into harbour, being unloaded, the dockers working, the carts of coal going up the hill to the railway and the great houses. His gardeners working in his own gardens; his estate cottages. Even when they were off-duty, his workers never knew when they were being watched.

'And he must've watched Henrietta as well . . .'

'How do you know all that last bit?' asked Aunty Megan sharply.

'Just guessed it,' said Uncle Geoff, and laughed. 'But I'm a good guesser. You know I always guess right.'

'I wish you wouldn't talk like that. You'll be giving Tracey nightmares.'

But when we looked for her, Trace had already gone, leaving the door swinging.

'Why didn't you *know* about Gower Park?' said Aunty Megan, even sharper. 'You must have remembered it, from when you were a boy . . .'

'Hardly. It was demolished in 1945. The Army had it during the War, and kicked it to bits. But it had been standing empty for years before that. I'd have only been two years old when it was flattened, thank God. Vile, isn't it?'

'What a horrible old man he must've been.'

'The year-book says that by religion, he was one of the Secluded Brethren. No fun for poor Henrietta. No dances or parties. No music, or singing or trips to London, or even Exeter. Just church three times every Sunday. Just the ugly great house, and the old man counting his brass. It's no wonder she wanted to elope with the first young man who asked her.'

'He wouldn't let her marry anyone who wasn't a Secluded Brother . . . would he?' Aunty Megan shuddered, and said, 'Come and have your tea. I don't think I want to hear anything more of the whole horrible business.'

But of course Uncle Geoff couldn't leave it there. It might have been better for us all, if he had. But historians are historians, and the following morning, old plans in hand, he set off to explore the long-forgotten kingdom he had found. And of course he wanted an audience, so I had to go with him. We left the Volvo in Gower Park Road, and trudged the interlocking shapeless streets of little bungalows.

Of course, now there was stuff to see everywhere. We even, on the main Exeter road, found the old gate-pillars of the Park, though the gates were gone. Massive and ugly and black they were, on the roadside verge. And we traced the avenue of chestnut-trees that must once have led to the Hall, stretching away into the distance across the network of tiny gardens. And huge blocks of black stone everywhere, and even a blackened, headless, armless statue of a muscular man, standing in a back garden. The gardener had

tried to train some ornamental ivy up it, without much
success.

We traced the site of the great house itself. The
thick stone garden walls of the bungalows grew higher,
as if the builder had been desperate to get rid of the
surplus stone at any cost; and most of the gardens had
sprouted large rockeries too. The little bungalows
looked as if they were perched in their puny cheek on
a great underground mass of stone; but that was all.

'Just one more thing to check,' said Uncle Geoff.
'There's a smaller house marked on this map, on the
crest of the hill. Part of the estate. Might've been a
dower-house or something, or the home farm . . .'

We shaded our eyes against the sun, and looked up
to the crest of the hill. And above the tile roofs of the
bungalows, all garish blue and green, was a higher
roof of honest dark grey slate. And a little tower and a
massive cluster of black chimneys, and a gable with a
church-like cross on the top of it.

'Glory be,' yelled Uncle Geoff. 'Whatever it is, it's
still there.'

And we both broke into a run.

By comparison with the old demolished hall, it was
small. But by comparison with the bungalows, it
seemed huge. As big as two big semis, two-storied, in
massive dark stone blocks. With a six-foot wall of
similar blocks all round, as if to keep out the view of
the barbarian bungalows, that surrounded it like
Indians might surround a covered wagon. A huge
pointed window by the front door, which was massive
and studded. The tower was three-storey, with battlements on top. And every room must have a fireplace,

and every fireplace a huge black barley-sugar chimney. The gate had tall black lamps on its pillars, but the glass was broken long ago. Inside the elaborate rusted iron gates, you could see that the garden had once been fine, with brick paths in intricate patterns, and clipped yews. But whatever garden plants were left had grown huge and high, trying to survive amidst strangling weeds.

'No time like the present,' said Uncle Geoff, bracing himself to charge in. I just wished he wasn't wearing his model-making trousers with the glue-stains, and a once-posh green cardigan that had a hole in one elbow. Still, he looked sort of noble in spite of it; he sort of rose above the clothes he was wearing.

We went up the overgrown path and knocked on the front door. The knocker was in the form of a grinning iron head, very rusty also. It made a terrible clumping noise, like something out of Castle Dracula.

I heard the quick approach of footsteps inside; I thought they were a woman's; and I suddenly wondered how on earth Uncle Geoff was going to explain his arrival in any way that would seem sane.

The door opened; a tall young woman with the most smashing legs stood there in very short shorts and a T-shirt marked LOVE YOUR NEIGHBOUR REGULARLY. She wore huge dark glasses, so it was impossible to see her face, except that she had beautiful lips. But her hair, black underneath, was surmounted by a star of platinum blonde strands above, spreading out from the crown of her head.

Somehow I was fairly certain she was not a member of the Secluded Brethren.

'Hi!' she said cheerfully. 'You'll be the antique-dealer's men?'

'Sort of,' said Uncle Geoff. His eyes were staring into the hall behind her, and he didn't seem to be quite with us. I followed his gaze.

There was a model ship standing on the chest of drawers in the hall. A ship about four feet long, including the bowsprit. A model of a collier-brig, in full sail. And the name carved on the stern, below the windows of the captain's cabin, was — *Nathaniel*.

'Wow!' said Uncle Geoff, and pushed his way past her a bit rudely, and went straight up to it. He fingered the rigging.

'Nice model.' His voice was trembling with excitement.

'They say it won't fetch much,' said the girl. 'They say it's too big to go into an ordinary house. They say there's no call for that kind of thing . . .'

'Who's *they*?'

'The dealers I've had in so far. From Stapledon.'

'Bastards,' said Uncle Geoff. 'Thieving bastards. Up to their old tricks.'

'I beg your pardon?' said the girl, her voice suddenly going a bit icy.

'How much have they offered you for this ship?' asked Uncle Geoff.

'Fifty pounds,' said the girl, a bit reluctantly.

'I'll give you double that,' said Uncle Geoff.

'Do you want to see the others?' asked the girl, a sudden warmth and interest coming back into her voice.

'Others?'

'This way,' said the girl, and opened a huge heavy mahogany door.

Beyond, there was sunlight and ships. Ship after ship; ships perched on deep window-sills, ships on sideboards, ships on shelves and even ships on the floor. All models of collier-brigs; I could see that. Same fat deep blunt hulls as the *Ebenezer*. Same black and white paint. Only, here and there, you could see differences. A shorter foremast; a larger mainsail. The *Reuben* and the *Joseph*; the *Rebeccah* and the *Rachel*; the *Isaac* and the *Blodwen*. All perfect, but very, very dusty.

'You can take the lot if you like,' said the girl. 'I hate them. I loathe this whole place and everything in it. That's why I'm selling up.'

Uncle Geoff looked round, a mixture of wonder and pain on his face. 'But why? The ships, the furniture, the house — all the same period and marvellous workmanship. It's like a time-capsule! It should be a museum.'

'What — a museum to Black Idris?' asked the girl. 'That's really *sick*. To hell with it — I'd rather have it chopped up for firewood. If you knew how many lives he's ruined . . .'

'Look,' said Uncle Geoff. 'If you can give me a bit of time I can get you far better prices than those thieving bastards from Stapledon will give you . . .'

'How?' She really was a modern girl. Blunt. Uncle Geoff was far older than her, and she showed no respect. I didn't like it. If they're all going to be like that when I grow up, I'd rather be a monk and live in peace and quiet.

'Sotheby's?' said Uncle Geoff. 'Christie's? These model ships alone would fetch a couple of thousand each at auction . . .'

'But you offered me a hundred for that one . . . what's your game?'

'I had to make you *listen*! I didn't want you selling to those Stapledon crooks.'

Something in his look seemed to convince her. She smiled and took off her sun-glasses for the first time.

'I'll believe you. You look OK for a golden oldie . . .'

'I'm only forty-six . . .' said Uncle Geoff indignantly.

'That's what I said — a golden oldie. Let's go into the garden and talk. I'll dig up some cans of lager.'

'I don't know all that much,' said the girl, taking a swig from her can of lager, and crossing her beautiful legs as she sat on the low wall. 'Black Idris is a sort of family legend. Came from South Wales, made a fortune grinding the faces of the poor, built Gower Park. He lived to be ninety — died in 1920. Ran his coal business to the end. The collier-brigs survived till the First World War. The War finished them. Worn out, sunk by U-boats . . . Then he just withdrew from the world and lived in the hall, and when he died, he left the whole place to my great-aunt Rachel. She was his granddaughter — the only relative who hadn't run away from him, as far as possible. Our lot — that's Ebenezer's lot — went off to Australia. Nat's lot went one further and fled to New Zealand. That's what they thought of Black Idris. They sort of trickled back here, when they heard Idris had finally kicked the bucket. But Aunt Rachel: she stayed faithful to the memory of Black Idris. Kept the Hall as long as she could afford to. Then sold up in 1945 and moved up here, with all his precious bloody boats . . . you know that every time he ordered a collier-brig to be built, he insisted the shipbuilders make a full-scale model, before he gave them the job . . . that's where they all come from.'

'Did you know your great-aunt Rachel?'

'I was brought to see her once or twice. She was just a dusting-machine. The priestess of his shrine. Never got married — never even had a boyfriend, even among the Brethren. He must have had her totally brainwashed. She only died last year, at the age of 88. What a bloody life to lead! She left the place to me, because I was a girl and still single. Tried to do to me what he did to her.' She shuddered. 'No way. This house totally spooks me. I've been camping out here for three weeks without proper heat and light, and I just can't wait to get rid of the furniture and leave it in the hands of house-agents, and get back to London. I'm an art-student at the Royal Academy School.' Her hand, holding the lager-can, shook, as if the cold of the house was reaching her, even out there in the warm garden.

'Look,' said Uncle Geoff, 'why don't you come and stay with us. I'm sure my wife would love to have you. And I could do the disposing of the antiques for you . . .'

Suspicion flared again in her face. 'What's in it for you?'

Gently, soothingly, he told her all about it. And her face, from being distrustful, grew still, absorbed. In the end, she said, 'You want to write a book about Black Idris?'

'Yes,' said Uncle Geoff. 'Perhaps I do.' I could tell the idea had just occurred to him; but he thought it was a good one.

'Why didn't you say so in the first place,' she said. 'I knew you had to be after something.'

'The family papers . . . portraits . . .'

'Be my guest,' she said. 'You're welcome to the lot. On condition that you tell the world what a bastard

Black Idris really was. None of that public benefactor crap. Give me half an hour to pack my things.'

She hurried off upstairs. Stealthily, like a thief, Uncle Geoff moved from ship-model to ship-model. Opening each big main deck-hatch, and groping inside. It was while he was groping inside the *Reuben* that I saw his face change.

'There's something,' he said softly.

And the next second, another tight-coiled roll of dull brown-edged paper was in his hand.

He took his time in reading it out to us . . .

Aunty Megan didn't bat an eyelid, when he turned up with a glamorous blonde in tow. I suppose she knew by this time that his interests were elsewhere . . .

But I don't think she was sure she liked that modern miss, Deborah Owen, at first. And by the time they'd stopped eyeing each other, and were really smiling instead, lunch on the terrace of Mount House was over.

It was only then that Uncle Geoff read us the letter.

'Different handwriting,' he said. 'Man's writing. Signed by our Humbert, no less.' He took a deep breath, and began to read it.

'My dearest love

Bad news. My father made another long journey to speak to yours, this morning. But the lodge gates were barred against him, and the lodge-keeper threatened to loose his dogs. My father says your father is a Blackguard, and he will not try to speak to him again.

We must take flight. It is our only hope, Far away, where he can never find us. There is a well-found ship, the *Brutus*, lying at Exeter Dock, bound

78

for Van Diemen's Land. She will leave next week, according to the weekly newspaper, when she completes her complement of cargo and passengers. We must be on her.

I have sold my books, and have the money for our fare. Your aunt's jewels, kept safe, should suffice to buy us a little farm and begin a new life, under the Southern Cross.

And I can always find pupils, if need be, I think, in such a new land.

I plan for us to meet under the Admiral, where we met that first joyous day, when the wheel of your carriage came off.

The day and the time, I will let you know later. I am sure your faithful Alan will help us.

Till we meet, when none shall ever separate us again, I remain,

Your worshipper and adorer,
Humbert.'

'Why . . .' asked our Trace, her head once again on her hand, in the style of Elizabeth Barrett Browning, '. . . was that letter still inside the galleon? Didn't she get that one, either?'

'Oh, I'm sure she did,' said Uncle Geoff. 'The *Reuben* wasn't shipwrecked like the *Ebenezer*. I'm sure she just kept the letter inside the *Reuben* because it was her safe place.'

Trace nodded. She knew all about hiding things in safe places. Sometimes her places were so safe, she forgot where she'd hidden things herself.

'Well,' said Deborah. 'I take my hat off to them. Anyone who could stand up to that old swine Idris . . .'

'But they didn't make it,' said Uncle Geoff dolefully. 'Humbert turned into the town drunk and was sent off to Canada, two years later. Alone!'

'So what happened to Henrietta?'

'We hoped you'd be able to tell us.'

'I never heard whisper of any Henrietta.'

'There's still your family papers,' said Uncle Geoff.

But he was still up to his elbows in family papers at the Dower House, still busy fending off the emissaries of the Stapledon antique-dealers with many an enjoyably-rude word, and ringing us up to tell us all about it, when we found Henrietta.

Or rather Aunty Megan did. She had set out to go round the Mountville branch of Sainsbury's, as she always did on Friday afternoons. There, she had heard two elderly blue-rinsed housewives being very catty about the Secluded Brethren . . . The simple thought occurred to her that Secluded Brethren must still exist. And that if they existed, they must meet for services, like any other strange religious bunch. They must have a chapel.

And the chapel might have a graveyard. And its own records, just like the parish church. She asked at the town Information Centre, and discovered that the local Brethren met at a chapel in the little village of Summergrove.

All this she told us over a cup of tea on the terrace.

Uncle Geoff was . . . miffed. He shuffled uncomfortably and said, 'Fancy you thinking to ask at the Tourist Information Centre!'

'Just common sense,' said Aunty Megan.

'I would never have thought of asking there!'

'Common sense was never your strong point,' said Aunty Megan.

Deborah Owen laughed out loud; which was not very tactful.

Uncle Geoff led the rush to the Volvo; muttering under his breath about some female Mafia . . .

It was another lovely evening, when we found the chapel. A plain little box with grey stone walls and small windows, almost like a barn. It was locked.

Uncle Geoff went off round the village to ask who held the key. Aunty Megan and Deborah began wandering around reading the tombstones while they were waiting — exclaiming about the great age of some granny who had died at ninety-seven; or mourning over some child who had snuffed it in 1878, aged five. The tombstones were very small and plain; but the grass between them was nicely cut. And like so many parts of the county, the land at Summergrove slopes down to the sea.

I didn't join in the tombstone reading. I sat on the gate, and watched the glitter of the sea to the west. The way the good ship *Brutus* must have gone, on her way to Van Diemen's Land. The ship poor Humbert and his Henrietta should have been aboard. Late bees buzzed past me, heavy with pollen and nectar. There was a nice smell from the fresh-cut grass, and a sourer one from the heap of grass-cuttings dumped by the gate.

I was thinking about the living and the dead, and about flying off into the sunset like a bird. The way it's pleasant to do on a sunny summer evening, somewhere high up with a good view. Such thoughts are not so pleasant on a wet Monday morning in term-time, and I normally avoid them then.

Suddenly my sister Trace appeared before me. She was so puffed-up with excitement and importance that she looked a bit like a frog. Her eyes were bulging with it. She could hardly speak. Then she nodded three times, like an old owl, and said, 'I've found Henrietta. Henrietta Mary Owen. She's *dead*. And she's buried all alone, on the wrong side of the church.'

We all stood around the grave solemnly, as if it was a small family pet that had just died. It seemed a very expensive grave, not at all like the others. It had a large and elaborate black marble tombstone, with anchors on it for some reason. There was a black marble kerb all the way round it, topped by rusty chains on spiky railings, and with marble chippings in the middle, up through which weeds were just starting to grow.

The tombstone looked stark and almost new, not like the others, which were all pleasantly moss and lichen. It reminded me of both the Dower House and the demolished Hall.

I thought miserably that Black Idris Owen had struck again. He had poor Henrietta fastened up for good now, and she would never get away to her Humbert or Van Diemen's land . . .

IN LOVING MEMORY OF A BELOVED
DAUGHTER
HENRIETTA MARY OWEN
BORN 13TH OF JUNE 1848
DIED 19TH OCTOBER 1866
'THE SEA SHALL GIVE UP ITS DEAD'

'Why's she buried the wrong side of the church, Uncle Geoff?' asked Trace for the third time. 'All on her own?'

'Perhaps . . .' said Deborah Owen, and stopped and blushed. She glanced at Trace and suddenly looked pretty upset.

'No, not that,' said Uncle Geoff hurriedly. 'If it had been *that*, they wouldn't have buried her in this churchyard at all, I don't think.'

'What does it mean?' asked Aunty Megan. '"The sea shall give up its dead"?' There were deep twin furrows in her lovely creamy forehead.

'She was so young,' said Deborah. 'Not nineteen. Far younger than me.'

'I'll tell you a funny thing,' said Uncle Geoff. 'And I don't mean funny ha-ha, I mean funny peculiar.'

We all looked at him and waited. He stood looking at the tombstone. Was he sad, or was he excited? You could never really tell.

'The interesting fact you don't seem to have noticed is that she died two days after the storm. Two days after she wrote that letter we found in the *Ebenezer*.'

'I don't like this,' said Trace, and shivered melodramatically, clutching her shoulders with both hands crossed. 'I want to go home. I wish I'd never come.'

I think we all felt the same. Except Uncle Geoff. I saw the glint in his eyes; the excitement of another mystery to solve.

I suppose Sherlock Holmes must have looked like that, when he was on the track of a murderer.

Except Sherlock Holmes didn't really exist; and my Uncle Geoff does.

Chapter Nine

The odd thing is the way we had a change of heart about Henrietta.

She became *our* Henrietta now. Almost one of our family. We all felt we had to find out what really happened to her, on the 19th of October, 1866. As Aunt Megan put it, 'It's just not natural, her being so full of life and hope one day, and dead two days after.'

'Perhaps he murdered her,' said Deborah. 'I wouldn't put anything past Black Idris . . .'

'He'd never have got away with it,' I said. 'They'd have hanged him, and they didn't. He lived till 1920.'

'A man of wealth,' said Uncle Geoff thoughtfully. 'There wasn't much they couldn't get away with, in those days.'

'Not in front of the child,' said Aunty Megan, warningly.

We all looked at Trace. Her eyes were like saucers; but she was still biting into a chocolate éclair from the tea-table, with enormous gusto.

What it boiled down to was that we all went every day to the Dower House together. Uncle Geoff said he could do with three more sets of eyes, because Black Idris's papers filled a whole room of dusty shelves upstairs. They went right from the beginning to the end of his life, and in the move from the Hall, they'd got hopelessly jumbled. I mean, we found his indenture as a ship's boy in the middle of a mass of rate-demands for his collieries from 1912 to 1920. And paper, on that scale, is terrifying stuff. A shoebox-full can eat up a whole day of your life, when you could be swimming on the beach. The dust gets up your nose, and the handwriting is hard to read because it's faded dim brown, and the printed stuff is printed so small, it makes your eyes jump like fleas. And you just know you're never going to find anything that means anything.

But worse than that was the house. Deborah was right; it did spook you. It sort of oozed Black Idris from every crack in the woodwork. The dark Victorian furniture, far too big for the rooms and crammed like a junkshop. It was like living with herds of shiny wooden elephants. And the pictures. Five of Black Idris himself. Black Idris as a ship's captain, with his brass telescope under his arm, and a storm at sea in the background. Black Idris as the mayor of Mountville, in scarlet and gold robes, when he was really old. But the rat-trap mouth was always the same, and the black beady eyes that followed you everywhere, and demanded to know what the hell you were doing, daring to be in his house. They got on my nerves; and Trace insisted on being escorted past them, when she wanted to go and play in the garden, or wanted to go to the loo.

We all huddled together in the kitchen to work; that was OK, just an ancient working kitchen. Great-Aunt Rachel must have spent most of her time there, and she might have been nothing but an old dusting-machine, but she wasn't half so bad as Black Idris.

But we still needed breaths of fresh air, and then we would go up to the top of the tower and stand in the sunshine, and let the breeze blow through our hair, blowing the cobwebs away. Or out into the garden.

Trace spent a lot of time in the garden. There was an old ship's figure-head stuck up on a wall; a jolly jack tar of some description, with a doll's painted face, and his striped arms folded, as if he was about to start to dance the hornpipe.

Trace spent a lot of time just sitting staring at it. Till the day I found she'd got a spade from some garden shed, and dug a great hole under it.

'What the hell you doing, Trace?'

'Looking for the treasure.'

'*What* treasure?'

'Henrietta's box. With her aunt's jewels. That was buried under the Admiral.'

I stared at the ship's figure-head with scorn. 'He's not an admiral. He's probably not even an able-seaman.'

'Is!' she said stubbornly.

'Isn't!' I mocked.

Well, it ended in tears, which was how the adults got to know about it. Then we had to all sit down and have a family pow-wow, to cheer Trace up.

'She's right, you know, Geoff,' said Aunty Megan. 'There was a box buried. By the faithful Alan. Under the Admiral. And when she died, it may have been all forgotten about . . . and those jewels. They mightn't be worth a fortune, but . . . if they're still there, they belong to Deborah here . . .'

'More likely the faithful Alan went back and made off with it, when the coast was clear . . .'

'Still, I think we ought to try to . . .'

'OK, I'll look into it,' said Uncle Geoff.

And with that Trace had to be content. Though she insisted on stowing a shovel in the back of the Volvo, and developed a nasty habit of wanting to stop at any graveyard we passed . . .

But by and large it was cold work at the Dower House, and back-aching and dusty and boring. Except, as Uncle Geoff said, you go on until you nearly give up, and then suddenly you find something, and a sort of electric shock goes through you; then it all becomes wildly exciting and you can't wait to get back to it.

Aunty Megan was the first person to find something.

An old brown music-case, full of torn-up photographs. We all sat on the floor, madly trying to piece them together, as if they were jigsaw puzzles.

Slowly, the faces of bewhiskered men and ladies with parasols grew and stared up at us.

'Who are they?' said Aunty Megan at last. 'And who tore them up and why?'

'And who kept them,' said Uncle Geoff, 'once they *were* torn up? And why?' Trust him to ask the really interesting question.

'I know who that is,' said Deborah, pointing to one photograph. 'And this one. Nearly all of them. My granny had copies of nearly all those photos. They're my ancestors. That's Eb — my great-great-grandfather. And that's Nat, who went to New Zealand.'

'But why tear them up?'

'Reckon Black Idris did that — when they ran away from home to the Antipodes because they couldn't stand him. He must have wanted to murder them — but all he could do was tear up their photographs.'

'Like Elizabeth Barrett Browning's father wanted to hang her dog when she ran away,' said Trace, never one to miss a chance to make a point about EBB.

'But who kept the pieces?'

'Somebody who still loved them . . .'

We were all silent, thinking about so much love and hate, so long ago. What did any of it matter now? They were all dead, lovers and haters.

Yet it did still matter.

I got the second break. Because Uncle Geoff was kind to me, and gave me the accounts-books of the steward of the Hall — the man who ran things for Black Idris, and bought things when they were needed. The entries were all short, in a neat crabbed hand, and were all dated, and rather fun.

'June 22 1862.   To a pound of butter . . . 6d
                    To three pounds of cheese . . . 1s.
                    To a pound of snuff for Mr I.
                      Owen . . . 5s.
                    To a good ball of string . . . 2d.
                    To six pounds of candles . . . 2s.'

Then I remembered about the fatal date, and went leafing forward through the dim brown pages.

'October 19th 1866.   To John Stratton, for three
                        loads of stones . . . 1s6d
                        To William Button, pavior
                        and mason, for repayring
                        the drive . . . 2s6d.'

I could have yelled with frustration. All those mysterious terrible things happening, and all the steward could think of was buying stones for repairing the drive . . . The next day, he was paying a man for digging potatoes, and a woman for two more loads of stones. On the next day, and the next, nothing. On the fourth day,

'For the ostler for seeing to Mr Owen's horses at Menning . . . 5d.'

And then, on the fifth day, there it was.

'To William Jones, Carter, for bringing home the body of Miss Henrietta Owen drowned, from the beach at Menning . . . 2s.

'For drink for the men . . . 6d.'

I showed Uncle Geoff, and he read it out to us all, and we were silent. Finally, he said, 'Menning is six miles west of here. The tide must have carried her right along there, for four days.'

'Drink for the men. The men who found her. After four days. She can't have been a pretty . . .' said Deborah.

'Not in front of the child,' said Aunty Megan. Then she said, 'So she drowned. But *why* did she drown?'

That's the way it is with research. You answer one question and raise a lot more.

That lunch-time, as we sat in the garden sadly eating sandwiches, Uncle Geoff raised the matter of Trace's treasure.

'I've checked,' he said, 'and there isn't an Admiral round here, above or below ground, this side of Plymouth. Besides, it's daft. If the Admiral had been alive, and moving about, you couldn't have buried *anything* under him. And if he'd been dead, and it had been buried under him, it would be six feet down. When you're in a hurry to elope to Van Diemen's land, you don't bury what you're taking with you six feet down. You bury it where you can reach it, quick.'

Trace's face fell. I think Uncle Geoff was trying to cheer us up; but he wasn't making a very good job of it.

'I've found the old coach route to Exeter,' he added. 'The old turnpike road. But it's hardly used now, since they built the Turton by-pass. No more than a country lane. But the funny thing is, while I was exploring it, I came across a pub called The Admiral.'

Now every eye was on his face; so he played his other joke.

'The trouble is, the pub wasn't built till the by-pass was, in 1955. It's in the middle of a modern housing estate. It was all green fields before that. Nasty-looking modern place. Hasn't even got a cellar, to hide a box in.'

'I want to see,' said Trace ominously, with a fearsome glare at him. 'I want to see for *myself.*' I could see there was a real tantrum on the way, if she didn't get what she wanted.

So could Aunty Megan. 'Oh, let's go and show her, Geoff. I could do with a drink anyway, with all this dust. Come on, you owe us one, for that.'

So we all went to The Admiral at Turton.

It truly was a ghastly place. It had just been re-modernised. It had a nasty white plastic cupola, with a fake antique clock, over the main roof. It sprouted plastic conservatories in all directions from its walls, like that disease that makes white blobs grow out of living goldfish. It had a car-park the size of a football pitch; blue sun-canopies over every window, advertising a famous lager; and a row of white plastic tables along the front, with sun-umbrellas advertising a competing brand of lager. The local farm-labourers had abandoned the plastic tables, and were sitting in the sun along the low wall of the car-park.

We sat at one of the tables, and Uncle Geoff went inside and ordered the drinks, and came out to join us. He was shortly followed by a young lad in an apron, carrying our drinks on a tray.

Uncle Geoff gave him a small tip and asked, 'Was there ever an older inn called The Admiral on this site. Before 1955?'

'Haven't a clue, mate. Only been working here a year.'

'Would you mind asking the landlord?'

'No use asking that silly bastard — he's only been working here two weeks.'

This got a loud laugh from the wall-squatting farmhands, most of whom were young, with hairstyles varying from John Travolta to Tracey Ullman.

Still, one of them shouted, 'Used to be another Admiral. Years ago.'

'Where was that?' yelled Uncle Geoff back.

'Up on the old road. Didn't do no trade up there, after they built the by-pass, so they pulled it down an' moved it here, where there's more boozers like us.'

This got a great roar of laughter.

But Uncle Geoff began to quiver like a whippet. 'Will you show me where?'

'Sorry, mate. I'm too short of drinking time. But it's up there a bit.' He gestured up a side road.

Never were drinks drunk so quickly. Trace drank

hers so quick the fizz got up her nose, and made her sneeze all the way there.

We found it. Or rather Uncle Geoff did. Where the side-road met another, he said to himself quietly, 'This is the old coach-road to Exeter. And that field is too small to be a real field . . .'

It was a field on the corner of the two roads; about an acre of scrubby miserable-looking land where nothing much grew but long dead grass and small bushes. There wasn't even a fence or hedge around it, just a few clumps of hawthorn. We walked onto it, and Uncle Geoff kicked at the long dead grass, and turned up something.

A damp half-brick. Then a damp whole brick, and underneath some crumbling wood and a smashed piece of dirty glass.

Uncle Geoff weighed the damp brick in his hand.

'That's a Georgian brick. Too long and shallow to be a modern one. This is the old Admiral all right. A coaching-inn where the coach stopped to change horses, and the travellers could have a bite to eat. The stable-yard's still here — look at these cobbles. And the stables would have been across there, away from the road. Look.'

And there was a low crumbling brick wall, with a rusted ring in it, for tying up the horses.

He showed us a lot. He even found the filled-in well which the horses had been watered from.

'It fits,' he said. 'It all *fits*. Only two miles from Black Idris's park wall — and there was a lodge with a back gate in that wall, right opposite here. And this would be the last stop for the coach, the last time it took on fresh horses before it reached Exeter . . .' He turned to us with eyes gleaming.

'This *must* have been where they arranged to meet. It all fits.'

'So where do we dig?' asked Trace.

Uncle Geoff looked round the acre site, full of shallow pits and depressions in the grass. 'Under the *Admiral. Under* the Admiral. It still doesn't make sense. How could they bury a box under a pub, or a stable-yard? And keep it secret, with all those people about, like ostlers, night and day? My God, Tracey, we could go over this site with twenty archaeologists, and a bulldozer, and still never hope to find it. Sorry, old girl. So near, and yet so far . . . Still we've got a bit more of the puzzle now, thanks to you.'

That didn't cheer up Trace at all, as you can imagine. She made quite a fuss. Uncle Geoff walked off across the road, to get away from it, and I went with him. That was where, kicking about, waiting for Aunt Megan to do her United Nations Peacekeeping Force act, we found the roots of a huge tree. The stump of the trunk was still there, grey and not really rotting, and six feet across, but now only a few inches high off the ground.

'Must have been a bloody big tree,' said Uncle Geoff. 'Oak, I should think. Must have stood for four hundred years.' I remember I did a kind of jokey tap-dance on the top of it, till Trace calmed down.

Then we all went back to the Dower House.

Chapter Ten

Two more days of slog, and everyone starting to lose heart and get snappy, and then came the *wonderful* day. I knew it was going to be at least bearable, because in the afternoon the bloke from Sotheby's was coming to look at all the stuff. E C Proby was his name.

But there we were, drooping round the kitchen on a rainy morning, and drinking endless cups of coffee because it was something to do. Uncle Geoff was buried in the details of Idris's Welsh mining business.

'Bastard,' he said. 'Posing as a public benefactor down here in Mountville, with his public library and public baths, but the things he was doing to his Welsh miners . . . letting little kids starve while their fathers were on strike.'

I was still mucking on through the steward's household accounts, but the price of bacon in 1897 had quite lost its charm. Tracey was singing a little song, or rather two little songs alternately. They both had only one line, sung over and over again. One line was 'I *do* wish it would stop raining' and the other was 'I am hungry I do wish it was lunch-time'. Aunty Megan was making some more cups of coffee.

Suddenly Deborah came in all flushed and triumphant and said, 'I've found another old music-case. And . . .'

She tipped out another heap of torn-up photographs.
Everyone piled into the jigsaw act.

And suddenly, there she was. Our Henrietta.

You couldn't have called her a pretty girl. Her face was too long and thin and . . . sad. Her lips were pressed together in a way that told you that she'd had a lot to put up with. You could see the marks of Black Idris all over her. Eighteen years of Black Idris. But she had beautiful dark eyes. Enormous eyes, still hopeful. And a very determined chin. Perhaps she had got the chin from Black Idris, but the eyes she must have got from her mother.

And best of all, there was one of her with her boat. It was big for a Victorian photograph, and you could see the details very clearly, even the name *Ebenezer*. The boat was lying in the water, across the stern of a big rowing-boat, and she was sitting in the stern-seat of the rowing-boat, holding the foremast of the *Ebenezer* delicately with one hand, to stop it floating away. She looked happy for once; she was smiling at the photographer.

And behind her, hunched over the oars of the rowing-boat, was another bloke, in a fisherman's jersey. A young bloke, little older than she was; but broad-shouldered, and with a stubborn yet adoring look on his face. From his clothes, you could tell he was one of the workers, and not a Victorian gent.

'The faithful Alan,' said Aunty Megan.

'I seem to have got the details of the *Ebenezer* right,' said Uncle Geoff. 'Only I should have made the mainmast a bit taller. But this was how Henrietta must have sailed it. From the back seat of a rowing-boat, just like we did.' Then he snorted. 'Black Idris

95

wouldn't let her go to dances, or have fun, but he let her sail his bloody model boats, because he was so proud of them. Serve him right if she used them to send messages to her lover, on the other shore.'

'Seems a funny way of doing it,' said Aunty Megan. 'Not very safe. Why couldn't she just send Alan round by land?'

'It's five miles round the estuary by land. Take him three hours, there and back. His absences might be noticed. Victorian servants didn't get all that much time off. And the boat must have seemed a safe enough way, if they all knew how to sail it. Even if Black Idris was watching through his telescope from his tower, a model boat going off course and being sent back by a helpful bystander on the far shore . . . innocent enough. It worked. Till the last time . . .'

'I'm going to mend all these photographs,' said Aunty Megan. 'And put them in a frame, at the head of our stairs.'

'There's something else in the music-case,' said Deborah. 'A newspaper-cutting. About a shipwreck. I wonder why . . . oh, it's from October 1866.'

We all crowded round; but the newspaper was very yellow and crumbly, and the print very small. So Uncle Geoff took it to the table and spread it out under a reading-lamp, and read it to us.

' "Dreadful Catastrophe — Loss of the *Brutus*.

' "It is with mournful hearts that we report the loss by shipwreck, last Tuesday the 18th of October, of the full-rigged ship *Brutus* with all seventy-one souls on board. She had sailed the previous midnight, with the tide, from the dock at Exeter, bound for Van Diemen's Land, and many people from this vicinity were on

96

board as passengers, with high hopes of making a new life in the Antipodes.

'"The day had dawned fair, with a gentle wind from the south, which promised a prosperous voyage; but there was a warning squall, still from the south, at about eleven in the morning, which drove many of the local fishing-boats to run for harbour, and threw some upon the sand, but fortunately without loss of life."'

Uncle Geoff lifted his head and looked at us. The reading-lamp threw strange shadows on his face.

'That was the squall that did for the *Ebenezer*,' he said and bent to his task again, adjusting his reading-spectacles.

'"Afterwards, the wind abated, only backing a little to the south-west; but there were many who, observing the sky, foretold that worse was to come. Nevertheless, the *Brutus* sailed at midnight, and made good time, it seems, past the estuary of the River Mount and on towards Plymouth.

'"However, it was observed by the local coastguard that the wind was backing more and more to the south-west, and rapidly strengthening to gale force.

'"At about four in the morning, blue lights were observed out to sea by the coastguard, followed by a discharge of distress-rockets, from the area known and feared by local fishermen as the Godwin Rocks, about a mile off shore. And with the dawn, a ship was observed, with bare poles and all sails blown away, fast upon those rocks.

'"The coastguard alerted the townsfolk of Mountville, and it is to the credit of the local fishermen that no less than four fishing vessels put out from the estuary, to attempt the mercy of rescue. Among those volunteering to man them was Humbert Vaux, the son of the lord of the manor of Mountville.

'"The vessels struggled under oars for several hours to reach the stricken vessel, for they were unable to raise sail, the gale, now of ferocious proportions, being dead against them.

'"At great length, they reached the vicinity of the doomed vessel, which was seen to indeed be the *Brutus*, and which was beginning to break up under the pounding of the waves, though many poor souls were still clinging to the wreckage.

'"The fishing boat with Humbert Vaux aboard went so far as to get alongside the wreck, under its lee and protected from the worst excesses of wind and wave. But at this point it was dashed against the breaking hulk, and capsized, throwing its crew into the waves, from which they were only rescued by the greatest good fortune, and valour of their fellow-rescuers, Mr Humbert Vaux sustaining injuries including crushed ribs, which fortunately have not proved fatal, but which will keep him bed-ridden for several weeks to come.

'"Soon after this, the wreck broke up totally, hurling many pitiable wretches to their death amidst the waves and rocks. In spite of the valiant efforts of the rescuing boats, only dead bodies were recovered, including those of several women and children. The boats then returned to the safety of harbour with their sad cargo, only escaping the perils of the increasing hurricane through the seamanship and valour of their crews.

'"Up to Saturday, only fifty bodies had been recovered, including those of the captain and the superior officers. Many were horribly mangled and in a state of nudity, after their pounding upon the mainland shore.

' "Another mournful loss reported was that of Miss Henrietta Owen, daughter of Alderman Idris Owen of Gower Court, who is reported to have fallen to her death from the cliffs to the west of Mount Castle, while witnessing the work of rescue." '

'Poor Humbert,' said Aunty Megan. 'All that bravery, and then coming back to find his girl dead in the same storm.'

'No wonder he took to drink,' said Deborah.

'And poor *Henrietta*,' said Trace indignantly. 'I wouldn't like to fall off a cliff in a gale.'

'That's what worries me,' said Uncle Geoff. 'I know that bit of cliff, beyond Mount Castle. It's a very safe cliff. I've climbed it, looking for gulls' eggs, when I was a lad.'

'What do you mean, a *safe* cliff?' yelled Aunty Megan. 'No cliff is *safe*.'

'It's very clean sound rock. Not at all crumbly. No loose soil or overhangs. And there's a low step just below the cliff top. If you fell off the edge, you wouldn't fall more than a few feet. And the wind was blowing from the south-west, a gale. It was blowing her *away* from the cliff edge. She'd have had to have been an idiot, to have fallen over that cliff . . .'

'Don't be so heartless,' shouted Aunty Megan. 'She must have been terrified. Humbert hadn't turned up for their rendezvous. Maybe she thought he'd gone without her, on the *Brutus*. Then people saying the *Brutus* was on the rocks, and then perhaps she saw him in the rescue boat, and saw the boat capsize . . .

she must have been nearly out of her mind with fear and worry . . .'

'That's what I'm afraid of,' said Uncle Geoff.

And there was an awful silence in the room, with Trace asking what Uncle Geoff meant, and nobody wanting to tell her.

And into all this gloom walked E C Proby. Brisk ring, ring, ring on the doorbell. I happened to be the one to answer it, and I couldn't believe my eyes. A willowy redhead in a black velvet trouser-suit, who didn't even look as old as Deborah.

'Yes?' I said.

'E C Proby, Sotheby's,' she said.

I led her into the kitchen, and announced E C Proby of Sotheby's. After all, why shouldn't I have some of the fun?

Everybody gaped except Deborah, who seemed to accept her as quite a natural occurrence. Uncle Geoff took some moments before it occurred to him he should shake hands.

'Sorry, I was expecting someone older,' he said gallantly.

'You mean,' said E C Proby, 'some bloke with a long grey beard and a yachting cap? Like Captain Birdseye, on the Fish Fingers advert on telly?'

Uncle Geoff had the grace to grin, ruefully.

'Well,' said E C Proby. 'If I tell you that that scale model of a schooner-rigged collier-brig in the hall there will quite possibly fetch over five thousand at auction, will you believe in me then? If I'm not mistaken, it's the sort that was made by the ship-builders apprentices for the approval of the prospective owner, and quite rare . . . one auctioned at

Sotheby Parke Bernet in New York last year fetched over ten thousand dollars . . .'

'Ten thousand dollars,' said Deborah, her voice rising to a squeak. 'But what about all the other ones in here . . .' She opened that door, and the even eyes of E C Proby went wide.

E C Proby accepted a coffee gracefully, when she finally agreed to sit down. But she still had her face in her black notebook, doing sums in her head. And she had several times mentioned 'The Idris Owen Collection'.

'You see,' she explained, 'you still have *everything*. Everything kept together. The models, the furniture of a shipowner's home, his accounts and letters, family portraits. It's a complete picture of a way of life. Unique; like a time-capsule.'

(Uncle Geoff nodded in self-congratulation at this point.)

'The more things are kept together,' said E C Proby, 'the more valuable they become. We shall contact not just wealthy collectors, but the museums, here and in America. There's a lot more money in America. Even the New York Yacht Club might be interested . . . or University Departments. When one starts bidding against the other . . . No promises, but we could be looking at well over two hundred thousand pounds, at the very least.'

'Just as long as they know what a bastard Black Idris was,' said Deborah. Then she stood up, with her eyes shining. Shining at Uncle Geoff.

'Oh, you darling!' she said to him. 'Those dealers at Stapledon weren't even going to give me five thousand for the lot. You could've taken advantage of me and made yourself rich.'

'Anything to do down those thieving bastards,' said Uncle Geoff. You could tell he was acutely embarrassed; he was actually blushing, and blinking like a morse-code lamp, and staring at his dirty old shoes.

Then she stepped up and took his face between her hands, and landed a great smacking kiss on his mouth, right there in front of Aunty Megan.

'Ah, it was nothing,' he said, with a very uneasy laugh, wiping off her kiss with the back of his hand, though I'm sure he didn't mean to be rude. I think he would have liked just to run away.

Aunty Megan was laughing her socks off. I sometimes think all women are in a great conspiracy against men, because E C Proby was laughing as well.

'I tell you what I'm going to do,' said Deborah. 'I'm going to keep my promise to you. You can have the *Nathaniel* for what you offered — a hundred pounds. Then you can do what you like with her — sell her and get rich, or go and sail her like a little boy.'

'OK,' said Uncle Geoff. He was still blushing, but he was laughing now as well. Only E C Proby looked a bit worried, at the idea of having a bit of her precious Idris Owen collection drift out of her reach.

Then we all went and had a drink and lunch.

Trace insisted, amidst groans, that we go to The Admiral. But everyone was happy, so she got her way.

It was raining harder as we drove to The Admiral, and the wind was getting up as well, driving sheets of rain against the windscreen, so that Uncle Geoff had to have the Volvo's windscreen-wipers going at their fastest.

We had to go inside, at The Admiral. Thank God it was pretty empty, because of the rain, but it was pretty grotty; there were electronic games pinging away to themselves, and a juke-box grinding out last year's hits, and a lot of red formica, and fake-buttoned leatherette. Yuk.

Still, it had its uses. The chips were good, and so were the hamburgers. And E C Proby looked so disgusted with the place that Uncle Geoff had to explain to her why we had to come there.

'A lady's box buried underneath The Admiral,' mused E C Proby. 'How very odd. As you say, The Admiral *can't* be a person or a pub. Could it be a monument? In memory of an Admiral?'

'The only one I know is the Hardy monument in Dorset. You know, Nelson's Hardy. Kiss-me Hardy. And that's nearly a hundred miles away. Ugly old thing — looks like a factory chimney. Built it for himself, when he was a retired Rear-Admiral.'

E C Proby sat silent and thoughtful. Then she said, 'It couldn't be a *tree*, could it? I remember watching a telly programme, when I was a little girl, about this great oak tree being cut down, that had stood for hundreds of years at a crossroads. It was cut down for a road widening scheme, I think. That was called the "Admiral" or the "General" or the "Captain". Something like that. There's quite a connection between retired naval men and oak trees. Their ships had been built of oak — "Heart of Oak are our ships", as the old song says. And oak was running short in England in the eighteenth century. Retired Admirals used to walk around with pockets full of acorns, and wherever they went, they made little holes in the turf with their walking-sticks, and popped an acorn down, to increase the nation's supply of oaks long after they were dead . . .'

I think she went on a lot more; she was a well-informed lady, E C Proby, in all matters historical and naval, and once she got her teeth into a topic, she was reluctant to let go.

But Uncle Geoff and I were no longer listening. We were remembering the great flat stump of tree across the road from the site of the old Admiral Inn. It all fitted. The inn named after the older oak. Perhaps the old inn-sign had been an oak tree, and not a stupid grinning pink portrait of Nelson, like the new pub had.

I was brimming over to interrupt E C Proby and tell her.

But Uncle Geoff caught my eye and gently held his finger to his lips.

It was to be our secret, till we found out whether the treasure was there or not. I think he didn't want to upset Tracey by building up her expectations.

When we got back to the Dower House, the rain had got even worse; and the wind, coming in sudden gusts, rocked the car.

We couldn't seem to settle any more, though. I think Uncle Geoff and I were too pent-up with the idea of that oak-stump, even though we couldn't do anything about it then. I mean, it was hardly the day to start digging something up. And I think he must have told Deborah about it, because she was restless too. And Trace must have picked up the restlessness, because her complainings grew worse and worse.

In the end, Uncle Geoff solved the problem for himself by suggesting that he show E C Proby the *Ebenezer* back at Mount House. They went off in E C Proby's car, and Deborah went with them, probably wanting to pump Uncle Geoff some more about the tree-stump. Their departure didn't cheer Trace up at all. She really knew that something was up, but couldn't get anyone to tell her, which is the thing that really makes her at her worst.

So Aunty Megan made the bright suggestion that she take Trace shopping at Sainsbury's, it being Friday afternoon and Aunty Megan's usual time for Sainsbury's. And there was tempting talk of nail-varnish and lipsticks . . . clever old Aunty M. She asked me if I would like to go along as well. But I was totally fed-up with Trace. So I said I would stay where I was.

'Your Uncle Geoff won't be long,' said Aunty Megan, as she ran for the car through the downpour.

Famous last words. How little she knew him! Uncle Geoff, given a chance to show off all his houseful of tricks to an expert from Sotheby's? Weeks wouldn't be long enough . . .

But I reckoned Aunty Megan wouldn't be too long herself. She doesn't enjoy Sainsbury's on a Friday afternoon . . .

I knew I'd made a mistake, the moment her car drove away. The house and its silence just closed in on me, like a vice. Black Idris seemed to come seeping out of every crack in the furniture, under the sound of the drumming rain on the roof. All those staring portraits of him; those little eyes peering at you, out of the green dusk of the rain on the windows.

I vowed to myself I would be grown-up. I *wouldn't* put the lights on . . . Ten minutes later, I put every available light on.

Then I wanted to go for a pee, and that meant going past *all* the portraits. Coming back, I found even the kitchen unbearable. The only room I could think of, that I could bear, was the tower room. It had great big round-topped windows, you see, in all four walls, so it was the lightest room in the house. And there was nothing in it, except a great big plain table in the middle, and four plain chairs set at it, and a plain wooden-board floor. Nothing of Idris Owen in it, at all.

So up I shot. I made myself walk up the first flight of stairs slowly and calmly, with the eyes of Idris the ship's captain boring into the back of my neck.

The last flights I went up like a rocket, and arrived panting and slobbering.

But the room *was* better; it did seem quite empty of Idris Owen. And the view was magnificent, out of those great windows. I could see, in the distance, through the drooping curtains of the rain-squalls, Mount House. The light was on in Uncle Geoff's study; a warm comforting point of gold in the grey-green gloom. He'd be in there, bless him, going on with great enthusiasm at his two young ladies. It was a warming thought; something to hold on to.

The only warming thought. Beyond Mount House, the clouds boiled across the sky; and the endless succession of waves crawled like curving black bars across a sea with the dull glint of pewter. Crawling endlessly towards the shore, the pattern ever-changing yet ever the same. And some waves boiling up the estuary and past me, making the weekend yachts bob and sway their masts, at the moorings by the Old Quay.

Then the great grey misty blob that was Mount Castle, property of English Heritage. Only it didn't look very English Heritage today; you couldn't see the information centre or the little ticket-office; it was just a great empty grey misty crag, without a person in sight.

And then more cliffs, and out to sea, a little dim distant flicker of white in the grey of the waves, where the fangs of the Godwin Rocks were, that ate up the poor *Brutus* so long ago.

I pulled up a chair to the big window with the rain running down it. And stared out. It was all so endless and ever the same, like the ticking of the great clock of the world. Down the window, raindrops chased raindrops, in endless succession, always the same, yet always a little different. In the sky, the boiling clouds heading straight at me were always the same, and yet always a little different. And the crawling waves of the sea . . .

I think that, hypnotised, I must have fallen asleep. For how could I have ever seen, at that distance, the tiny sail of the *Ebenezer* bravely crawling across the waters of the estuary, till she was embraced and swallowed by the sand? How could all the silly white bungalows be gone, and the great black Hall sprawling again on the green cliff top? With the tower of Idris Owen stark and high against the sky, and a tiny figure on top, telescope raised to his eye, watching, watching?

How could I have seen the flicker of two galloping horses through the rain, heading for the back lodge and gate in a park wall that no longer existed? Or the shattered masts of the *Brutus* hard fast on the Godwin Rocks?

Or, later still, the figure in a white dress on the cliff top beyond Mount Castle, sitting her horse in the rain, with a dim faithful figure on a second horse, respectfully a little way behind her?

A figure in a white dress and dark cloak that looked, not out to sea, but beseechingly inwards, towards the land? As if hoping and hoping that *someone* would come for her?

Yes, it was impossible. Yes, I was asleep and having a nightmare. For afterwards I heard Trace's voice say with gladness, 'Here he is. Fast asleep, the lazy thing!'

And I felt my cheek pressed flat against the cold and clammy glass of the window. And Trace told me afterwards that I said, on waking, 'Who is she waiting for? Why is she looking towards the *land*?'

Yes, it was only a nightmare. Too much had happened to me that day, too quickly. Or else it was the cheese in my cheeseburger at lunch.

Chapter Eleven

I think we did the oak tree business all wrong. It was Uncle Geoff's fault.

We went in broad daylight. Uncle Geoff had something he called an archeological probe: two feet of steel rod, with a sharpened point at one end, and a big broad handle at the other. (He made it himself in his workshop in half an hour.)

Even before we'd got to the site, he and I and Deborah, we'd worked out the box would be buried *behind* the oak tree, out of sight of the turnpike road and the inn, which must have been only about thirty yards away. So nobody passing could see what was going on. Uncle Geoff reckoned it wouldn't be buried deeper than a foot.

When we got there, we saw there were only two gaps between the remaining great roots, where a box of any size might have been buried. We all squatted down.

'If anybody asks,' said Uncle Geoff, 'we're doing a nature-study. Looking for seven-spot burnets ...' Then he thrust the probe into the damp earth. It went down surprisingly easily, with a thin squeak, just grating against the occasional stone. Five or six times it went in, right down to the handle. You could tell there was nothing there. My heart sank slightly; I began to feel we were behaving like silly day-dreaming children.

Uncle Geoff moved across to the other gap, and thrust down again.

Immediately, there was a crunch. A bit like breaking wood, and less than a foot down.

'*Got* it,' muttered Uncle Geoff. 'There's a hollow here. Then something soft.'

I gave him a nudge with my elbow then, because a dirty and battered Land-rover had just pulled up across the road, where the inn used to be, and I knew he hadn't seen it.

A bloke got out; he wore an open-necked shirt, an open waistcoat and a flat cap, so I reckoned he must be a farmer. He walked across like he owned the place.

'What you doin' on my land?'

Then Uncle Geoff looked up and he and the farmer said, almost together, 'Oh, it's *you.*'

They obviously knew each other. They equally obviously disliked each other. And yet it was a polite dislike, as if they both knew they had to go on living together in the same town. Adults are funny that way.

'Oh, it's you, squire,' said the farmer again. And it wasn't quite rude, because the Vauxes *have* been squires around Mountville for hundreds of years.

'Oh, hallo, Wally,' said Uncle Geoff. 'Still busy fiddling the EEC?'

'Stupid Froggy bastards,' said Wally cheerfully. 'They're trying to cut my milk-quota again.'

'No doubt you'll find some other way of cheating them.'

Wally laughed shortly and harshly. He made no attempt to deny it. Then he said, 'What are you doing on my land?'

'I would have thought,' said Uncle Geoff calmly, 'that this was part of the road verge, the public highway . . .'

'Only up to the oak tree . . .'

'We are looking for seven-spot burnets.'

Wally's little blue eyes blinked rapidly. He obviously hadn't a clue what seven-spot burnets were, but he equally obviously had no intention of admitting it. Instead, he looked at the archaeological probe in Uncle Geoff's hand.

'What you going to do wi' that,' he asked. 'Spear them, or batter them to death?'

'They're grubs in the earth. Like leather-jackets.' Uncle Geoff could lie without even blinking.

'Oh,' said Wally. He obviously knew what leather-jackets were. 'Well, if you find any, just remember they're *my* seven-spot burnets you're nicking. Meanwhile, *I've* got real work to do.'

And he got into his Land-rover and drove away.

'Damn and blast,' said Uncle Geoff. 'It would have to be *him*.'

That was how the whole thing turned into a full-scale commando operation. Aunty Megan thought we were mad. But we turned out, Uncle Geoff and Deborah and I, dressed in dark clothes and with blackened faces, at two o'clock on the Sunday morning; Uncle Geoff having carefully rung round his friends to find out Wally's Saturday night habits.

'He'll be in bed by this time,' said Uncle Geoff, 'with a skinful of real ale. Dead to the world. And he won't be up till six to milk his cows.'

'Isn't this all a bit melodramatic?' asked Deborah. 'I mean, the stuff *is* mine. She was *my* ancestor.'

111

'Not under the law of treasure trove,' said Uncle Geoff. 'Wally Warburton would try to make some claim as owner of the land. He'd certainly make a fuss in the courts. It could drag on for months and months, and cost a bomb, even if he lost in the end. He's like that. The number of people he's sued over the years . . .'

'I feel like a thief,' said Deborah. 'Stealing what really belongs to me anyway.'

Uncle Geoff had it all worked out. He dropped Deborah and me by the oak with the gear, and drove off to park the Volvo half a mile away, near the new Admiral. Deborah and I lay low behind the oak stump.

'I've always wanted to be out in the countryside in the middle of the night,' said Deborah. 'But you never get round to it. It smells lovely. We might see badgers. Did you hear that noise? Is it a fox barking?'

Uncle Geoff was back in ten minutes. 'Get behind that bush over there,' he said to Deborah, 'and tell me when anyone's coming. And you get back up the side road,' he said to me.

I lay and watched the road, and listened to him digging with his army entrenching tool. The smell of fresh-dug earth came drifting to my nostrils, to join the smells of damp grass and trees. I confess I was wriggling with excitement. Occasional cars kept sweeping past, even at half-past two in the morning, making a great scythe of light with their headlights as they turned the corner; and showing up the hump of Uncle Geoff's bum quite clearly, as he flattened himself behind the oak stump. But they all passed on; even our local police, which nearly gave me a fit.

Perhaps they thought Uncle Geoff's bum was a curi-ously-shaped stone . . .

But about three, by the luminous dial of my watch, it seemed to go all quiet, except for the odd white barn owl sweeping across as silent as a ghost and making Deborah squeak with fright.

'Right,' came Uncle Geoff's muffled voice. 'Got it. But the wood's very soft. Come and see.'

We beetled across. There was, by the light of his tiny torch, a flattened mound of fresh-dug earth, a hole, and in the bottom of the hole, a small wooden chest with a curved top. He'd done a lovely job, an archaeologist's job, which can't have been easy, work-ing in pitch darkness. But there were still ominous signs. One iron-bound corner of the chest had col-lapsed into a pile of rust-fragments; and where the probe had gone down yesterday, there was a star-shaped hole in the curved lid, and a crack that ran from one side to the other.

'I wish we could have taken photographs,' said Uncle Geoff, 'of every stage . . .'

'Oh, for God's sake get *on* with it,' said Deborah. 'Before we all end up in Exeter nick.'

'You sure?' said Uncle Geoff, suddenly doubtful.

'What else have we come for?' said Deborah.

'Right,' said Uncle Geoff. 'I didn't want to force the lock but . . .'

He reached down and tried to lift the lid.

It crumbled in his hands like old cake. One minute there was a rounded top; the next minute just piles of soft fragments dropping out of his hands.

An awful smell of rotting rose to our nostrils.

'Oh, God,' said Deborah. 'It's awful. It's like opening her grave.'

The earth had not been kind to Henrietta's box, as the sand had been kind to her ship.

Uncle Geoff picked away the lumps of crumbling wood. Each piece crumbled into smaller pieces as he lifted it. It was just a mess.

'What's all that brown stuff?' asked Deborah.

'Clothes, I think. I can see a bit of lace collar or something.' He lifted it; but it, too, crumbled away. 'It's *hopeless*.'

'The jewels might have been in some sort of little box . . .' said Deborah. 'Go *on*. What have we got to lose?'

'There is a smaller box.' Uncle Geoff's big hands were just scooping out the rotten cloth in handfuls. He picked up a square object, and it too crushed to pieces in his careful hands.

But we caught the flash of something falling.

'Was that a pearl necklace?' gasped Deborah. 'With something on the end of it?' She grabbed for it; lifted it in triumph.

The string that held the pearls together must have broken. Tiny points of soft light scattered in all directions amongst the crumbling rubbish. We all tried to pick up the ones we could see; but I know we didn't get half of them.

We searched a long time, through the ever-crumbling rubbish. The sides of the box had caved in by then. It was just *chaos*. Nothing else worth having.

'I can't bear this,' said Deborah. 'It *is* like desecrating her grave. Fill it in. I want it filled in again.' Her voice went shrill, like she was going hysterical.

Uncle Geoff sighed, and began shovelling the earth back. After all, it was Deborah's box . . .

Two more cars passed, before we finished and put

the turf back. One of them was the police car again. How awful, to be arrested for *nothing*!

But it didn't see us, and drove on.

Uncle Geoff went off for the car.

'I feel I've done something terrible!' said Deborah, her voice muffled against the earth. 'We've desecrated her memory. All for *nothing*.'

But it wasn't quite for nothing. As we sat back in the kitchen of Mount House, drinking cocoa and being glad not to be in Exeter nick, Uncle Geoff pulled something out of his pocket. Something about an inch across and two inches long, an oval that glinted gold.

'A locket,' he said. 'That was on the end of that string of pearls. Real gold.'

The locket, being gold, opened fairly easily. Gold survives anything.

On one side was something that might have been a painting of a young woman's face; once. On the other side, the lid clicked back to show something that might once have been the painting of a young man.

Even the paintings were crumbly; even inside the locket the damp of a century had done its worst.

'I'll not open it again,' said Deborah. 'But I'll keep it for ever in memory of them.'

We made a little pile of the pearls we'd managed to rescue. Deborah said she'd have them restrung, as a bracelet for Trace. So she would have her treasure after all.

'Surely there must have been more than that,' said Uncle Geoff. 'More jewels. One pearl necklace and gold locket wouldn't have bought a farm.'

'Maybe the faithful Alan went back afterwards and helped himself,' said Deborah. 'Who's to blame him? As long as it didn't go back to Idris Owen.'

Chapter Twelve

It was the last day of our holiday, really. Tomorrow, we would pack to go home. Deborah was going too; back to London. Sotheby's had cleared the Dower House, and the 'For Sale' board was already up in the jungly garden. There was talk of turning it into a small private nursing home. I pitied the old people who would have to endure it. Not nice to spend your declining years in the company of Black Idris . . .

Uncle Geoff had been working like stink on the Owen papers, before Sotheby's took them too, and they passed out of his reach to some museum in the Atlantic Seaboard. The previous night he had finished with them, late. Now, he threw the vast heap of photocopies into a corner of his study and said he felt like a day out.

And for him, the day out meant sailing his new ship. Deborah had been as good as her word, and sold it to him for a hundred pounds. She and Uncle Geoff were as thick as thieves. But Aunt Megan didn't seem worried. She said that after three sons, Uncle Geoff deserved to have a daughter for a bit. Which remark left our Trace considerably miffed.

Uncle Geoff and Barney had been over every inch of the *Nathaniel* and pronounced her fit to sail, without restoration. Over the last hundred years she'd suffered

116

from nothing worse than dust and tobacco-smoke. Barney reckoned she'd be faster than the *Ebenezer*. Uncle Geoff reckoned she'd be slower.

Today we'd find out. Even Aunty Megan had joined in the party mood and produced a picnic basket, saying we were bound to end up somewhere we could eat a picnic, even if it was just our own cove.

We all trailed down to the beach. It was the hottest day we'd had, and Uncle Geoff and Barney agreed the wind would be tricky. It was light, SSE, but it kept gusting, then falling quiet. No danger of a storm. But complications caused by the shape of the cliffs. And the chance of alternate land and sea breezes, as clouds crept over and shadowed the land.

Anyway, we rowed out, in our usual positions, but with Deborah sitting on the boat's bottom, up beside Tracey in the bow. She was getting a bit splashed by the oars, and there was a bit of water washing to and fro in the bottom of the boat, but she took it in good part, and said it would help keep her cool.

Uncle Geoff decided to sail the *Nathaniel* across our cove first; towards the beach below Mount Head. Barney was allowed to set the sails. Into the water she went.

In the gentle breeze, she sailed like a dream. She *was* faster than the *Ebenezer*.

'That's five quid you owe me,' said Barney.

'She's better at reaching,' said Uncle Geoff, as if he hadn't heard him. It's not that he's mean about paying his debts, he just hates to be wrong . . .

As I said, the *Nathaniel* sailed like a dream; until we got close to the cliffs of Mount Head. We followed her with a lazy plash of oars, knowing that even if she beat us to the beach, she'd be in no danger of damaging herself today.

It happened when she was about ten yards from the beach. I don't think it was anything supernatural — just a tangle of moving air, caused by the wind rebounding off the cliff. But she suddenly swung round to face us; as if she were a dog waiting for us, hesitating, impatient.

Then her sails swung over, the wind filled them, and she was coming straight back at us, on the other tack. Moving much faster now, running with the wind from the sou-sou-east behind her.

We should have caught her; but Uncle Geoff and Barney got in a muddle with the oars turning the rowing-boat, then they were afraid of hitting her with an oar, and she shot past us, her bow-wave bright bubbling creamy-white, leaning hard over, every sail drawing perfectly, asleep.

She headed straight past the rocks that had caught the *Ebenezer* and out into the estuary.

I've never seen Uncle Geoff and Barney row so hard. We *had* to catch her; thousands of pounds of antique boat flying loose, and in the estuary it was the weekend, with yachts and power-boats coming and going all the time, and any one of them could run her down without even noticing her . . .

Jeepers, we weren't going to catch her. The wind had veered again, to south-east, and she was starting to run past the cliffs below Mount Castle, on the far side of the estuary, and out into the open sea. In the vague direction of the Godwin Rocks. Sweat ran down Barney's face; Uncle Geoff's face was pure agony. Trace was screaming her head off and Aunty Megan was making sarky remarks under her breath about men playing like little boys and that damned boat would fetch enough money at auction to buy her a new fitted kitchen.

Past Mount Castle now, and the sea-waves starting to rock us too. We were gaining on the *Nathaniel* a little, but she was still thirty or forty yards ahead, and going better than ever. Uncle Geoff and Barney were running out of steam and the *Nathaniel* wasn't even trying, yet. If the wind freshened any more, she could sail as far as Plymouth. If she missed the Godwin Rocks . . .

And then the wind swung back towards the south. As if there had been a tiny helmsman on board, the *Nathaniel* altered course again. Towards a little cove that I had never seen before, that lay just beyond Mount Castle.

As she neared the beach, the back-draught of the wind bouncing off the cliffs caught her, and she came upright, and idled around in a hesitant circle, as if she had only been fooling with us, and now she was sorry.

We were very glad to get her back on board; she dripped coolly on my bare legs.

And by the time we had got her on board, we were almost on the new beach ourselves.

'Let's take a breather,' said Uncle Geoff. 'I don't know about you, but I could do with a can of lager.'

So we beached the rowing boat, and carried the *Nathaniel* up on to the sand for safety. The idea of her escaping again, while our backs were turned, was unbearable.

Uncle Geoff and Barney stood sipping their lager from Aunty Megan's cool-bag.

'Nice little cove,' said Barney. 'Very quiet.'

'There doesn't seem to be any way down from the cliff top. Some coves haven't got one, you know.'

'Not a place to be caught at high tide; unless you've got a boat, like us. Wonder who it belongs to? Not a crisp-bag or a lollipop stick in sight. If I lived in Mountville I'd come here often, to get a bit of peace.'

'They don't want peace,' said Uncle Geoff. 'They want amusement arcades, or villas on the Costa Brava.'

'Suits me.'

'It must once have belonged to Gower Park,' said Uncle Geoff. 'We can't be far from the Dower House, here.'

And suddenly I shivered; like somebody had walked over my grave. I looked up, half-fearing to see a figure in a white dress and blowing cloak, standing up there, among the crannies of the cliff's edge, dark against the sky.

But there was only blue sky, and little drifting white clouds.

Then Aunty Megan started to unpack the picnic gear, because Uncle Geoff wanted a sandwich. And after that, somehow, it turned into an early lunch, even though it wasn't even half-past eleven. And then, what with the heat of the place and the sun and the food and the lager, all the adults went dozy and just wanted to lie and sunbathe. Adults are infuriating like that. I mean, all day to explore, and a marvellous boat to play with, and all they can think of is snoozing and nattering in lazy voices.

I lay back in disgust, and closed my own eyes against the sun . . .

And then Trace was suddenly poking me.

'Wake up, dope. There's a funny red thing on the cliff. I can't climb up — it's too dangerous. *You* do it!'

What a thing is sisterly love! But I went with her. It was the only way to get any peace. No, that's not fair. I was curious myself.

The thing was about ten feet up the cliff, in a sheltered gully. Well above the high-water mark, but the spray had done its worst, and the object was red with rust, glowing strangely bright in the sun, against the sombre dark rock of the cliff. In shape, it was like a very fat cross. And it wasn't wreckage; it seemed to be bolted to the rock.

It was quite a scramble getting up. I nearly fell once, which would have been quite painful, and very embarrassing.

Close to, I tapped it. It was a thick plate of cast iron. It seemed to have lettering on it, but the rust made the lettering hard to read, like the lettering above the door of Mount House. In the end I had to read it out to Trace by feeling with my fingers; spell it out letter by letter.

'IN LOVING MEMORY OF'

It was a cast-iron memorial. Like the one I'd once seen, half-way up Striding Edge, on the mountain Helvellyn, in the Lake District. That one was in memory of some climber who fell at that spot and broke his neck. Not a gravestone, but a memorial. That one was kept well-painted. The Victorians did that kind of thing sometimes. At the place where the accident happened . . . Trembling now, I read on with my fingers.

'IN LOVING MEMORY OF
HENRIETTA MARY OWEN

DIED 19TH OF OCTOBER 1866
IN A FALL FROM THIS SPOT.
HAVING WAITED TWO DAYS
FOR HER FATHER OR HER LOVER
TO FETCH HER FROM THIS PLACE
AND THEY PROVING FAITHLESS
IN DESPAIR SHE CAST HERSELF DOWN.
THIS MEMORIAL IS PLACED BY HER
GRIEVING FRIEND ALAN
REST IN PEACE.'

I dropped down the cliff, and Trace and I looked at each other. She nodded her head. As if she was very sad, but also satisfied.

'I wonder how he knew she waited two whole days before she jumped,' I said.

'Because he was there, being faithful, right till the end, I expect,' she said. 'I hope I get somebody as faithful as that. Like Elizabeth Barrett Browning.'

Suddenly, I took her seriously for the first time. That look on her face. I could imagine how she would look when she was grown up. Even when she was quite old.

'You *did* it, Trace,' I said. 'You kept us at it. The picture on Mary's stair, the treasure under the Admiral. You asked the right questions . . .' I was rather amazed, actually.

'That's cos I'm interested in *people*,' she said. 'You and Uncle Geoff are only interested in *things*. Things are no good without *people*.'

Then we called the others. When Aunty Megan read the memorial she said, 'Oh, what a waste of a young life, to jump like that. Couldn't something have been done? Couldn't people have been told quickly enough to save her? Couldn't somebody have told her Humbert was hurt and couldn't come?'

Uncle Geoff said, in a low voice, 'Perhaps she was beyond telling. We can never know what went through her mind. But she must have been terrified of her father and his power. And she must have felt damned, an outcast, with everyone against her, after what she had done. And she must have thought either Humbert was dead, or had rejected her . . . she no longer had anywhere to run to. So she just lingered, then she jumped.'

'Couldn't the faithful Alan have done anything?'

'Perhaps he got her back to the Admiral to sleep, one or both nights. But what else could he do? He dared not leave her side for a moment. Perhaps he was terrified, paralysed, too. Old Idris had the whole district paralysed. Like some Nineteenth Century Stalin. After all, Alan was only a servant, and servants were kept pretty crushed in those days.'

'Only one person could have saved her. That bloody old man,' said Uncle Geoff. 'He must have known she was there. He must have known she had nowhere else to go. And he sat in his tower doing nothing. When I write my book, I'll *crucify* him.'

Then he said, 'Now we know what faithful Alan did with the treasure he took from the box.'

I hate saying goodbye at railway stations.

It would be a whole year before I saw Uncle Geoff and Aunty Megan again. I wished I could live with them always.

But perhaps it wouldn't be so good, if I lived with them always. Perhaps I'd get tired of them, as tired as I was of what I was going back to. My mother, brown as if she'd been to the Costa Brava, sitting at the word-processor knocking off endless statistics about child-deprivation in Indonesia. My father, raising his head with smiling weary patience from the talk he was writing for the World Health Organisation about the use of human excrement for fertilising vegetables in Hong Kong. How worthy, how infinitely dull is doing good wholesale. Like Sainsbury's sell cheese . . .

If my father was good, was Uncle Geoff wicked? Caring for nothing but crumbling old clocks and weapons and documents, riding his wild black rides back into the past? Which was more important, the starving millions of Asia, or Henrietta Owen and her brave fight for freedom?

My father would have no doubt; my father never seemed to have any doubts.

I grinned at Uncle Geoff, and beckoned him forward and whispered in his ear, 'I'm going to be a *bad* Vaux when I grow up.'

He stepped back and grinned his wicked old grin, and waved as the train drew out.

Tracy sang her one-line songs, all the way to London.